MURDER IN ALL FURY

ANNE CLEELAND

ARTEMIS
PRESS

THE SERIES IN ORDER:

Murder in Thrall
Murder in Retribution
Murder in Hindsight
Murder in Containment
Murder in All Honour
Murder in Containment
Murder in Misdirection
Murder in Spite
Murder in Just Cause
Murder in the Blood
Murder in Deep Regret
Murder in Revelation
Murder in Unsound Mind
Murder in Material Gain
Murder in Immunity
Murder in All Fury

For Moo, whose ways are the ways of gentleness; and for all others like her.

CHAPTER 1

athleen Doyle sat in the comfortable armchair, feeding baby Tommy and thinking about nothing in particular—as one tended to do in a dark and quiet house, when everyone else was abed. They were on holiday at the present time—an unusual occurrence, since neither Doyle nor her husband, Lord Acton, were what you would call holiday-taking people. But Acton had suggested that they visit the seaside whilst she was on maternity leave and she'd readily agreed—mainly because he wouldn't have suggested it unless he'd wanted to go, himself. He needed a bit of peace and quiet, poor man; he was still on-end about the Public Accounts scandal, which had taken-up so much of their lives lately.

She shifted the baby to her shoulder, and—leaning back in the chair—sleepily began to pat his back. Tommy was down to one feeding a night, which was a blessing, even though she didn't mind—not truly; there was something to be said for such an elemental experience that no one else could share, save the two of you.

Sunk into the soft recesses of the chair, Doyle hadn't realized that she'd fallen asleep until she saw—with some surprise—that she'd a ghostly visitor, here in the nursery. Doyle was what the Irish would call a 'chime-child'—fey; and born with an extra-perceptive sense that was sometimes useful and sometimes a major annoyance, depending on the circumstances. In her day-to-day life, Doyle's perceptive ability allowed her to read the emotions of the people around her, and she could usually tell when someone was lying, which was a useful sort of talent for a detective, even as it meant she didn't tolerate crowds very well. And—as part-and-parcel of this extra sense—she would dream about ghosts, on occasion; rather persistent ghosts, who tended to give her advice.

When this phenomenon had first begun—several years ago, after she'd first married her husband—she'd been dismayed by the ghost-visitors, but now she didn't mind them as much—mainly because experience had shown that she'd best have a listen. Doyle's wedded husband tended to be involved in some heavy doings—not all of them above-board, unfortunately—and oftentimes the ghosts seemed to be tasked with giving her some sort of warning.

This time, the ghost was a man in his early forties—a familiar figure, who regarded her with a benign expression as he seemed to hover, suspended above the nursery floor.

"Oh," said Doyle. "I'm that sorry you're dead."

"I'm not sorry," Nigel Howard replied, and smiled.

"Acton's furious about it," she disclosed.

"Wrath," the ghost agreed. "There's good reason that it's one of the seven deadly sins."

"Don't I know it." Doyle and her husband were detectives at Scotland Yard, and tended to see the wages of wrath on a daily basis—or at least usually she did, being as at present she was on maternity leave.

As her visitor seemed disinclined to explain why he was haunting her, she assured him, "People are goin' to prison for it—for your murder I mean. The trial is comin' up very soon—it just took a bit of time to get it all lined-up."

Howard had been an MP, and he'd uncovered a massive embezzlement operation within the government bureaucracy—the Public Accounts scandal. The panicking bureaucrats—once they'd become aware that he was on to them—promptly arranged for his murder, using a tainted shipment of over-the-counter drugs so as to disguise their true intent.

"When you think about it," the ghost noted, "vengeance is just a variation on wrath."

Strangely enough, this seemed to imply that the ghost did not necessarily approve of the criminal justice system—which would be a fair point, if he now had a bird's-eye view of heavenly justice. Still and all, it seemed a rather odd thing to say and Doyle explained, "Well, the trial is right around the corner. We can't just let people get away with murder—and it's deservin' of a bit of vengeance you are, my friend."

"Exactly," he agreed, with a small smile.

Puzzled, she stared at him. "Exactly, what?"

"Avenge my death." He paused, and then added politely, "If you would."

Doyle blinked. "But—we're doin' just that; the CID has rolled-up all the villains, I promise you."

He tilted his head in mild disagreement.

Very much surprised, she ventured, "There's people that are goin' unpunished?"

"Yes. I wouldn't ask if it weren't important."

But—thoroughly confused—Doyle disclaimed, "I'm not the

proper one to ask, to go about doin' vengeful things. Acton's the vengeful one, not me."

"Exactly," he said again, and seemed well-pleased by this insight.

With some alarm, Doyle cautioned, "But please don't go hauntin' him—he's on a hair-trigger as it is."

"Avenge my death," the ghost repeated. "If you would."

And then Doyle was startled awake, staring at the empty room with her heart hammering in her ears as the baby slumbered, undisturbed.

CHAPTER 2

I've got to stop having babies, Doyle thought a bit glumly. It tends to send my poor husband off the deep-end.

She'd risen early to complete the baby's morning feeding—with only the one night-feeding, it meant the morning feeding came early—and now she sat at the breakfast table, idly watching out the window and hoping to get a glimpse of Acton as he returned from his walk. It was a beautiful view; the house used to be an inn—The Mermaid Inn, the housekeeper had said—and it was situated on a bluff overlooking the ocean.

Doyle found herself staring at the waves, unblinking, as they hypnotically rolled onto the shore, and contemplated the rather dismaying fact that Acton had experienced yet another restless night. Between her husband, the baby, and the ghost, Doyle was in sore need of a cup of strong coffee, if only she'd the energy to get up and make a pot.

The isolated house was near to Burnham-on-Sea, which was, in turn, near to Bristol. She and Acton had talked—from time-to-time

—about going on holiday to Brighton, but Doyle's husband had decided there was not enough privacy in Brighton, and so now they were tucked-away in this old Georgian house—close enough to the sea to hear the waves at night. Apparently, the place used to be an inn for smugglers and pirates, back in the day, but it was now a fancy bed-and-breakfast with an altogether different clientele.

And it was somehow appropriate that they were staying in this pirate-house, on a windswept bluff, because Acton was simmering something fierce; he hadn't been sleeping well, despite the relaxing sound of the ocean, and often he'd get up at night and go walking for hours on end. It was very unlike him; in the usual course of events, he was attached to her like a barnacle, and rarely stirred a step from her side.

Mayhap, it's not having the new baby that's driven him off the deep-end, Doyle consoled herself; mayhap it's the fact he doesn't much like being on holiday—and after all, it would be miles easier to avoid going on holiday rather than avoid having children, going forward. Although he'd a similar rough spell once before, when their eldest child was born; he'd the same sleepless nights—got a bit paranoid, and was not his usual self a'tall.

Not that his "usual self" was easy to define, of course. Doyle's husband was the wealthy and celebrated Lord Acton, famous for his work as a Chief Inspector at Scotland Yard, but—despite this public persona—he was not at all what he seemed to his legions of admirers. He battled demons, did Acton, and—although the wife of his bosom was able to smooth him out a bit—she knew there was much he kept from her, probably for fear she'd run screaming off into the windswept moors herself.

And now—now a ghost was giving her a call-to-action and she hadn't the least idea how to go about it—not to mention that she felt as motivated as a limp wash-rag, and had a baby who was more-or-less permanently attached to her bosom.

But the ghostly call-to-action was something she shouldn't ignore, as she'd well-learned from past experience. Sometimes she knew the ghost from life, and sometimes she didn't, but a clear pattern had emerged with respect to the dream-ghosts; there was good reason that this particular ghostly person had shown-up to deliver a message, and she'd learned—sometimes the hard way—that she should pay close attention.

This one, of course, was something of a surprise—although, to be fair, that was the whole reason for the ghosts; that she wasn't aware of something important, and she needed a bit of a nudge.

Nigel Howard had been murdered in a brutal scheme that saw nine innocent people also killed to hide the fact that he was the intended target. A batch of over-the-counter drugs had been laced with a deadly dose of fentanyl, so as to make it appear that the manner of death was a quality-control mistake by the pharmaceutical company. Doyle and Acton had managed to solve his murder, and now the villains who'd been behind the scheme were facing trial and a lifetime in prison—the villains being a group of government bureaucrats who'd been caught skimming public money.

Although—for reasons that were unclear—apparently, the CID was on the wrong track, with this one—or at least, that's what the ghost was strongly implying. But how this could be was a true puzzler; the circumstances of Howard's murder seemed straightforward—faith, more straightforward than many of their other cases, truth to tell.

Howard was the MP who'd initiated the investigation on the Public Accounts case—which took a bit of bravery, since he was apparently one of the few government officials who was not directly profiting from the corruption. Therefore, when he'd unexpectedly died, his death had aroused immediate suspicion; it seemed a bit too convenient that the fearless reformer had died, and by such a random accident.

Subsequent events had proved this suspicion correct, and the motive soon became obvious; the blacklegs had caught wind that the boom was about to be lowered, and—in a panic—had concocted this tainted-medication scheme so as to take him out. Not only that, but the scheme had been carefully crafted to obscure the motivation behind it, with nine other random people murdered also, so as make it appear to be mere negligence.

So; why would Howard's ghost think that CID was on the wrong track, now that the villains had been arrested and were about to go to trial? It made no sense.

Although—come to think of it—Doyle had been a bit surprised that the bureaucrats had managed to pull-off such a finely-wrought scheme. The defendants in the Public Accounts case may have been greedy, but they didn't seem to be much in the way of masterminds—particularly as they'd been fairly easily caught-out in their embezzlement rig, with no ready explanation for the large sums of missing money. Faith, even your average mafia kingpin knew enough to siphon-off money in small amounts so as to set off no alarms.

So; there must be more to this than met the eye, and the fair Doyle should shake her stumps, and figure-out why Nigel Howard was haunting her dreams and demanding vengeance. It was very unlike him, after all.

With a knit brow, she continued watching the waves as she considered this point—since it seemed a good one. Howard was the last person—one would think—who'd be calling for bloody vengeance; he wasn't a scorched-earth vengeance-taker like Acton was. Acton had murder-in-the-blood, due to his ancestors' tendency to smite-down anyone who looked at them cross-eyed; it was an unfortunate failing, but there it was.

By contrast, Howard had been an unassuming, rather gentle man in his life—in fact he'd been a bit discouraged by the many compromises he'd been forced to make, in his attempts to make reforms. As a result, he'd seriously considered stepping-down from politics and instead creating a non-profit organization, so as to try to implement the reforms he'd hoped for—he'd always been a peacemaker. A peacemaker, who was now politely asking that the fair Doyle avenge his death.

These rather troubling thoughts were interrupted by Mrs. Mackey, the local housekeeper, who greeted Doyle in a cheerful tone as she entered the kitchen,and set down her things. "Good morning, Lady Acton; how is that baby?"

"The baby is excellent," Doyle declared "Never better."

Mrs. Mackey was an older woman—forthright, and no-nonsense—who'd come along with the house-rental. She'd been rather surprised to discover that Lord and Lady Acton hadn't brought along their nanny so as to help with the children, but Doyle had assured the woman that no help was needed.

Indeed, it had been something of a nice respite for Doyle. She came from a working-class background, and—although she'd now grown accustomed—it had been a bit difficult to adjust to a life with servants who were always underfoot. And so it was rather nice, these past few weeks, to have things whittled-down to just her little family—with its brand-new member—whilst she found her feet. Not to mention that it was a blessing to have fewer people about to notice that Acton wasn't himself. With a troubled gaze, Doyle looked out along the shore again, hoping to catch sight of him.

Mrs. Mackey followed her gaze out the window as she bent to

light the stove. "It looks to be a beautiful day—a bit warmer, I think."

"It does, indeed; I'll see if Acton wants to take Edward along the beach, again—although I don't know where we'll stash yet another bucketful of wretched sea shells."

The woman chuckled. "He will lose interest, never fear; and then you can dump them out again when he's not looking."

"Well, I hope he loses interest before he brings them home to Reynolds. Although I suppose Reynolds would only think of somethin' clever to do with them, like re-pave the hearth."

At Acton's suggestion, Reynolds, their butler, had taken this opportunity to enjoy his own holiday—which presented a rather amusing picture, since Reynolds wasn't the type to wander off sporting a guidebook and a camera. But the capable servant deserved a break and this seemed a perfect time, with the rest of the family holed-up here, at the seashore. They'd hired a new, full-time nanny—Miss Valerie—but she hadn't been included in the trip. Nor had Trenton, their security-man, which was a testament to how much Acton wanted to pare the staff down to the bone. No matter; with Mrs. Mackey to handle the cooking and washing, it had all turned out very well.

As the housekeeper began to assemble the breakfast, she offered, "My Jamie might go over to the Marina, this morning—he wants to find out more about the fire."

Doyle suddenly stilled, as she continued to stare absently out the windows. "Was there a fire, then?"

"Oh yes—in the Marina. It's been on the local news."

Doyle confessed, "I haven't listened to the news, lately—I'm too busy bein' a milk-cow. Tell me about it, if you would."

"It was last night, over at the Heaton Marina." Mrs. Mackey made a derisive noise. "The rich folks' yachts, getting burned-up."

"Now, that is a shame," Doyle said, and was rather gratified that her companion did not lump her into the aforesaid rich-folks category.

The housekeeper lowered her voice. "They are saying they found a body. They don't even know if it's a man or a woman, because it is all burned-up."

There was a small pause. "I'll be needin' some coffee, please," said Doyle.

CHAPTER 3

*D*oyle was mid-breakfast, when Acton came in, taking off his jacket as he greeted Mrs. Mackey, and then coming over to kiss his wife and run a fond hand over Tommy's sleeping head. "How is everything?"

"Everything's grand," Doyle replied. "We've a few more minutes of quiet, I think, before Edward smells the bacon and wakes himself up."

"I am just in time, then."

He settled into the chair beside her, and Doyle asked, "How went your walk?"

"Very invigorating," he replied, and nodded his thanks to Mrs. Mackey as she poured his tea.

"Did you scout-out any seal carcasses?" This, because they'd come across one the morning before, much to Edward's ghoulish delight.

"All clear, toward the north."

"Good; we'll have to head that way, today."

In a desultory manner, she fingered her coffee cup. "Is the

Heaton Marina within walkin' distance? We could go take a gander; Mrs. Mackey says there was a fire there last night."

Acton nodded in acknowledgement. "Yes. In fact, the local station-house has asked that I attend a briefing because they believe there may be a connection to the Public Accounts case."

"Is that so?" asked Doyle, who found that she was not at all surprised. "Well—there's a wrinkle. Smugglers?" she guessed.

It was a time-honored tradition that those who wished to avoid scrutiny at Britain's entry ports would use private yachts— or even fishing-boats—to transport contraband. And—as though to illustrate this point—the Public Accounts case had uncovered a network of various operations that served to pass along laundered money, often in the form of artwork and coins, in and out of Bristol.

Doyle already knew quite a lot about the workings of the smuggling network, mainly because the man sitting beside her had helped to set it up in the first place. Not only did her husband have murder-in-the-blood, he also had raid-the-coffers in his blood, and—in his defense—it must have been so very tempting to have such sums of money being overseen by a bunch of dopey bureaucrats. It would be easy pickings for the likes of him.

Naturally, his law-abiding wife was horrified by the discovery that Acton had a questionable hand in setting up the wide-reaching embezzlement rig, and so he'd promised to put a stop to his unlawful doings and make a renewed effort to walk the line, going forward.

But—obviously—walking the line wasn't working out so well. Doyle may be tired, and by no means a mastermind like her husband, but she was not so dim that she didn't see a connection between her ghostly visitor, Acton's restlessness, and this mysterious smuggler's fire.

"Yes—it seems evident that the yachts were used for

smuggling," her husband agreed, as he thanked Mrs. Mackey for his plate. "They made regular circuits to France."

"Why the fire, I wonder?" Doyle feigned idle speculation, but was actually focused like a laser-beam on her husband's reaction. "A fallin'-out, amongst thieves? Do they think it's arson?"

"They do. The first suspicion was insurance fraud, but when they began interviewing dock personnel the local authorities discovered the smuggling connection, and the possible link to the Public Accounts case."

"May I tag along, when you go?" she asked with an air of innocence. "The dock personnel may be in on it, and I could nose-out anyone who's coverin' up." Doyle's husband was well-aware of her ability to recognize lies when they were being told, and they often used this talent to good effect on many of the cases they worked together.

He tilted his head. "There's a Code-Twenty, I'm afraid. They've asked if I could help with the possible ID."

A Code-Twenty was a burnt body, which was not something for the faint-of-heart. On the other hand, there'd been at least one occasion where a Code-Twenty had been manipulated by Doyle's wedded husband to hide the fact that the decedent was not actually the person who'd been identified. Acton was someone who knew his way around an arson fire, unfortunately.

She didn't dare press it, however; half the reason she tended to catch-out her wayward husband was because he didn't realize how much she knew, or had guessed.

"I'll stay home, then," she said easily. "A shame, though; I'm that ready for a chance to walk twenty paces altogether without various small children hangin' onto me."

"Perhaps we will return home soon."

She nodded, rather relieved. "Aye—it's very pretty here, Michael, but all this peacefulness seems to be rubbin' you the wrong way. I don't think you do well, away from your natural habitat."

There was a small pause. "You may be right," he agreed.

So; he wasn't going to take the opportunity to tell her about whatever-it-was that was bothering him, which was only in keeping; Acton kept himself to himself, and in the past he'd rarely stirred a step from his flat in London—which had only added to his mystique as the brilliant and reclusive Lord Acton, solver-of-crimes.

And it only went to show the mighty, transforming power of love in that—wonder of wonders—he'd abruptly decided to marry his support officer, and allow her entry into his carefully-guarded world. As a direct result, the reclusive Lord Acton now had two sons, various nannies, and a wife who wouldn't leave him be when it came to his natural inclination to mastermind and skirt the law. Although to be honest, it seemed fairly clear she wasn't doing a very good job of steering him aright; after all, boats were burning and ghosts were haunting.

Reminded, she asked, "Has the trial date been set for Howard's case? Poor Mary, to have to live it all over again."

Mary was their former nanny, who'd met Nigel Howard with the two falling instantly in love—even though he'd been engaged to a pretty aristocrat at the time. It was a tragic sort of fairy-tale, though; Mary and Howard had married, and had just welcomed a baby daughter when tragedy struck with Howard's death. It was one of those times when you truly questioned how you could possibly be expected to "give thanks, in all things" even though you were, and no bones about it.

Acton replied, "The Plea and Trial Preparation Hearing will be held day after next, and I'd thought to invite Mary for a visit here, with your permission."

With all gratitude, Doyle immediately fell-in with this plan.

"Now, there's an *excellent* idea, Michael. We'll distract her, and Edward would love to see Gemma."

Mary had a stepdaughter—a few years older than their Edward—and no doubt it would be a welcome break for Mary and Gemma to visit the seashore for a day or two, and avoid the publicity of the murder trial's preliminary hearing.

Of course, Doyle knew that her husband had another motive aside from sparing Mary's feelings; the wife of his bosom was in need of her own distraction. He knew she was aware that something was troubling him mightily—they knew each other very well, after all—but she'd learned, long ago, that if Acton didn't want to tell her something there was little chance of winkling it out of him. And so—because she'd an impressive record of winkling things out, with or without his cooperation— he'd decided to keep her occupied with something else.

Which was all in keeping with what the ghost was hinting at; it seemed a fantastic turn of events, but apparently the suspects who'd be in the dock at Howard's trial were not the ones who were actually guilty of the murder. And—in light of this yacht-fire, and her husband's strange and distracted mood—she'd bet her teeth that Acton was already aware of this rather troubling fact.

Which meant that time was short, for the fair Doyle to figure-out who the true suspects were and bring them to justice—even though she hadn't the least idea how to go about it, being as she was currently wearing her mother-hat and would not be donning her detective-hat any time soon.

With a small sigh, she called out to Mrs. Mackey. "Another cup ma'am, if you don't mind."

CHAPTER 4

$\mathcal{A}$cton had gone in to the Bristol station-house for his meeting and then returned after lunch, just in time to join Doyle and Edward for a beach-walkabout.

With some excitement, Edward held up his bucket. "We'll get more shells, da."

"I think you can never have enough," his father agreed, and swung him up so as to carry him down the steps to the beach. "Which way are we headed?"

"Away from the dead seal," his wife reminded him.

"Right. This way."

With Tommy sleeping soundly in Doyle's chest-carrier, they set out along the beach, and Acton threw a fond arm across Doyle's shoulders as they watched their son dare the waves to touch his feet.

"I'd tell him not to get wet, but that's a faint hope," Doyle noted. "It's a wonder he risks a dunkin', what with the water so cold."

"Nothing that a hot bath won't cure."

"No—that's half the reason to chill yourself to the bone; a hot bath feels like heaven."

They walked along for a few paces and then Doyle asked, "Did you ever go to visit the seashore, growin' up?"

"My mother has relatives in Anglesey, and we'd visit, from time to time. Not the same as this—the shore up there is quite rocky."

She teased, "I don't know which sounds grimmer—your wretched mother's relatives or the bleak shore."

He smiled slightly, but didn't respond—which was only to be expected; he didn't like talking about his life growing up, being as it had been something of a horror-show. Doyle had often noted that her own youth—lived with a single mother and in hard-scrabble poverty—had been miles better than her husband's, despite his vaunted title and his luxurious estate.

With some sympathy, she offered, "Your relatives are lucky that you didn't behave like that fellow in the famous story—the one who pulled the pillars down and destroyed everything out of vengeance."

"Samson?"

"No—not a Bible story; the story where the fellow was a bit dodgy, and did a lot of broodin'."

Acton considered this, as they walked a few more paces. "I'm afraid you may have to be more specific."

She laughed, and replied, "Well, the 'broodin' hero' one I'm thinkin' of is the one I was forced to read in school, since it was 'literature' and such. The girl wouldn't have him and so he went away to make his fortune, and then came back to take his revenge. Faith, but it was a slog—depressin' as all-get-out, and glum as a miser's wake." Brightening suddenly, she remembered, "There was a ghost, though—so at least there's that."

"*Wuthering Heights?*"

"That's the one, Michael—faith, but you have a head like an encyclopedia."

"I will confess that I quite enjoyed the story."

Laughing, she acknowledged, "*Of course*, you did—you and your wrathful self; you probably thought he wasn't dodgy a'tall, but instead was a righteous hero."

Shaking his arm in remonstrance, she reminded him, "Kindly recall that things didn't work out so well, for him. There's good reason, that wrath is one of the seven deadly sins."

He smiled. "Then you must never spurn me, and we will never have to test it out."

"Not a chance, my friend; you are well-and-truly stuck with me." She lifted her face for his kiss, and—thus reminded—offered with a show of enthusiasm, "And speakin' of such shall we give it another go, tonight?"

Doyle's libido was going through a dead spell—a similar thing had happened after Edward was born. She chafed at it, because— aside from the fact that she very much enjoyed sex with her husband—when one of Acton's black moods was hovering, a hearty bout of sex was just what was needed so as to pull him out of it.

And a black mood was definitely hovering, she admitted to herself; even though this time it wasn't the usual situation. In the usual course of things, Acton's black moods were triggered by some cataclysmic event—usually wrought by him, truth to tell— and they were rather short-lived, with Doyle frantically trying to keep the fallout to a minimum. This time, however, he seemed to be continually simmering at a low pitch for days unending, and it alarmed her a bit. It wasn't good for him to be so—so *angry*, and the worst part was that she was at a loss as to why this was.

Usually, the reason was evident; someone had crossed him,

and that someone was slated to pay a terrible price unless Doyle could appeal to Acton's better angel. This time, however—unless she very much missed her guess—he was unhappy about the Public Accounts case and how it had landed. Small wonder, that her antenna had quivered when she'd heard about the burnt-up yachts; something was up, and Acton was teetering on the verge for some reason.

Which made it all the more annoying that her usual lust for her handsome husband had disappeared, just when it was sorely needed to distract him from whatever-it-was that was fretting him to pieces. She'd made an effort, the other night, but it hadn't gone very well—being as her husband had a very fine-tuned radar when it came to his wife, and he'd known that the spirit may have been willing but the flesh was overwrought with having produced a baby, and was therefore taking a break.

He rested his head against hers, and said with some sympathy, "Not on my account, please. I am content to wait until you are fit for duty."

"Sorry," she offered, feeling foolish.

"Whist," he replied, teasing her.

"Look!" Edward shouted in wild excitement. "A dead seagull!"

"Holy Mother," said Doyle.

"Don't touch it, Edward," Acton called out.

"Another faint hope," said Doyle.

"I will find him a stick," Acton suggested, and then walked over to accomplish this task.

Doyle watched them, and—because she's stopped moving—the baby began to stir in his carrier. She jiggled him a bit, whilst Acton and Edward poked about and discussed the finer points of dead birds at some length.

They finally resumed their walk, Edward leaving the bird's

corpse only with great reluctance. As he ran ahead of them, Doyle offered, "Mayhap he'll be a coroner."

"I doubt he will do anything that requires standing still."

She decided that she may as well ask, "Speakin' of such, how was your Code-Twenty?" It had not gone unnoticed by the fair Doyle that her husband had made no mention of his visit to Bristol.

"No ID as yet. Pelvic structure indicates a woman. Teeth and jaw indicate Caucasian—perhaps Slavic."

This was of interest—that it was a woman—and Doyle suggested, "Mayhap it's Charbonneau, finally turnin' up like a bad penny." One of the blacklegs from the Public Accounts case— a woman—had mysteriously disappeared several months back.

"Perhaps."

She glanced up at him. "You don't think so, though."

"I don't think she's the right height, for Charbonneau— although we can't be exact, of course."

Seizing this opportunity to do a bit of probing, Doyle ventured, "Seems a bit odd, that someone from the Public Accounts case would want to silence this victim, if that was indeed the motive for the arson. You'd think there'd be no one left to do the silencin'; all the major players have been rolled-up."

But he only pointed out in a mild tone, "Motive is as yet unclear. It may well have been an accidental death."

"Alcohol?" Doyle asked.

"They couldn't do a preliminary screen; there is not much remaining."

She glanced up at him. "I'd be that surprised if this was an accidental death, Michael—it seems too big a coincidence, and you're the one who's leery of coincidences. Instead, I think someone wanted this poor victim silenced, for some reason, which leads me to believe that there's a suspect or two in the Public Accounts case who may have slipped the net, and are tryin' to keep it that way."

"There is always that possibility," he agreed. "We'll first need an ID, though, before we can look at known-associates."

"Aye—there's the rub, I suppose."

Doyle let it go, because she'd already discovered what she was probing for; when she'd mentioned uncaught suspects, her outwardly-calm husband had quickly suppressed a mighty flare of alarm. So; this seemed to confirm that Acton knew whatever-it-was that the ghost knew—someone had got away with Howard's murder. And—if this burnt body was indeed connected to the Public Accounts case—then that selfsame person had probably committed this grisly murder, as a topper.

Strange, that Acton didn't just say so—didn't tell her outright what he thought was going forward. It led one to believe that he was covering for the murderer, which didn't bode well. After all, Acton was the one who'd first set-up the Public Accounts scheme; could it be that he was covering for someone so that his own role would not be revealed?

After considering this troubling theory for a moment, she discarded it; Acton was far too clever to allow himself to be left at the mercy of any paltry bureaucrat. Not to mention that if anyone tried to accuse him, they'd be laughed out of the Crown Prosecutor's office; it was one of the reasons Acton got away with the things he did—no one would believe for a moment that the illustrious Chief Inspector dabbled in major crimes on the side.

So; if he wasn't covering for this murderer so as to protect himself, then why was he covering? And how was this unknown woman's murder connected to Nigel Howard's call for vengeance? Because it was, of course—it had to be; Doyle knew it, down to the soles of her shoes.

I'm stymied just now—what with being on maternity leave, she thought; and so, I'll just have to be patient. Which is a shame, because patience isn't my strong suit.

"A dead crab!" Edward shouted, and Acton dutifully left her side so as to go have a look.

CHAPTER 5

*T*wo days later, Doyle was waiting in the front courtyard for Mary to arrive with her children, whilst keeping a weather-eye on Edward as he demonstrated to baby Tommy—who was lying on a blanket and kicking his feet madly—the proper way to jump off a stone wall.

Her mobile phone rang, and—thinking it was Acton, who was upstairs working—she answered it, "Ho."

"Doyle? Sorry to bother you."

It was Officer Gabriel from the CID, and Doyle knew a moment's surprise that he would call her during her maternity leave. "Hallo, Gabriel—don't you dare get promoted whilst I'm sidelined."

"Too late," he advised.

She smiled; Gabriel was a friend and rather mysterious, in that he'd been shunted from intelligence work at MI 5 over to the CID when they'd been short-handed, and then—rather surprisingly—he'd stayed. Truth to tell, she wasn't even certain of his rank; she only knew that he'd had her back in many a tight corner and could be considered a staunch ally.

He asked, "Any chance you'll be back in the office, soon?"

"Not for a few more weeks." Ominously, she warned, "Don't you dare give Munoz all the good assignments in the meantime."

"Munoz is currently in Ireland, I believe."

"Oh—that's right." Munoz was Doyle's main rival for assignments and promotions, and at present the other detective was on holiday, visiting her Irish husband's family.

"I did want to touch base with you, if it's possible."

He's worried about something, she realized; now, that's interesting. "We're headed back by week's-end, I think, so long as Acton doesn't decide to throw it all in and set-up a stall on the boardwalk to sell trinkets."

"I'd only envy him his low-stress job."

"Chin up, Gabriel; I'll come by to show you the baby. Now, there's a de-stressor like no other—he's adorable."

"Great—let me know. Sooner, rather than later, if you don't mind, lest I be having to set-up my own stall on the boardwalk."

"Aye, then; I wanted to ask you for a favor, anyways."

"You did? This sound ominous, and I may have to rethink my request."

"Too late," she advised, and rang off.

I wonder what that's all about, she thought, but before she could dwell on it the driving service arrived to deliver Mary and her two girls, and all rational thought had to wait in the flurry of greetings and shrieking children.

The first order of business was to head to the beach, and so— once the two babies were put down for a nap—Mrs. Mackey packed a picnic lunch which was fated to go largely ignored, as Edward and Gemma raced off to play in the water.

Doyle and Mary followed at a more leisurely pace, and then decided on a likely spot to roll-out the blanket. They settled-in to unpack the luncheon and keep watch over the children—not such a hard task, for Doyle, since when Gemma was with him Edward tended to be less reckless.

"Gemma's been so excited," Mary said to Doyle, as she watched them run away from the waves. "Thank you so much, for having us."

"Whist, Mary; I'm bored to flinders."

Doyle paused, much struck, because this was true; she wasn't cut-out to be idle, and it was past time she was back to doing what she did best—unwinding human tragedy. And keeping a sharp eye on her husband, of course, which was part-and-parcel of the aforesaid unwinding.

And—speaking of such—now that she'd been alongside Mary for a small space of time, she was aware that the young woman was very unsettled—brimful of conflicting emotions, was Mary. Doyle was fairly certain she'd soon hear the reason why; Mary was about as good as Doyle at keeping her own counsel, which was to say she wasn't very good at all.

More mysteries, she thought; between Gabriel and Mary, I'm to be put through my paces today.

Mary noted in a somber tone, "Nigel's preliminary hearing is today."

In sympathy, Doyle touched the other's hand. "I know. Best be away from it, I suppose."

Her companion grimaced, slightly. "The Crown Prosecutor thinks that I should attend the trial, though."

Gently, Doyle pointed out, "It does make a difference, if the jury sees the grievin' widow. If they see only the repentant defendant, it tilts the pitch a bit."

Mary nodded in resignation. "I know, and I owe it to him—to Nigel. I just hate thinking about it—about the press, and how aggressive they've been. Philippe says he will sit next to me, and if any of them tries to ask a question he will knock them down."

"The jury would love it," Doyle declared. "Talk about tiltin' the pitch."

Anyone else might be forgiven for thinking that Philippe Savoie was an unlikely hero, save for Doyle. Savoie was a notorious French criminal kingpin who'd been happily minding his kingpin-business on the Continent until a few years ago, when he'd come over to England because he'd suspected that his Russian partner-in-crime was doing him wrong. This little visit had resulted in the Russian partner—a man named Solonik— winding up dead, with Savoie deciding that he'd like to stay in London for the nonce—much to the dismay of the Home Office types, who nervously watched his every move.

Doyle was fairly certain that the reason Savoie had decided to linger in London, was because he and Acton had managed, somehow, to team-up on various enterprises that couldn't withstand the light of day; guns-smuggling, for one, and this Public Accounts scheme, for another. The two men were rarely seen together—Acton was a respected Chief Inspector, after all—and her husband took great pains not to let Doyle catch wind of their collaboration, but even her wily husband was no match for Doyle's intuitive sense.

The recent unraveling of this Public Accounts case had resulted in Acton's confession that he'd set-up the original scheme with Savoie's assistance, and so his unhappy wife had made him promise that he'd never dabble in such a thing, again. After all, she was supposed to be a police officer—so was he, for that matter —and it was outside of enough that he kept breaking the law, and with no thought to possible repercussions.

But there was no way to know whether Savoie had sworn off, too—she'd no control over him, even though they were friends.

Savoie was a complicated man—much in the same way that Acton was a complicated man—and there was no telling why he did the things he did; as a result, Doyle had long abandoned any attempt to try and make sense of him.

As a case in point, the Frenchman had saved the fair Doyle's life, a time or two, and for this reason she knew that Acton felt beholden to him. Savoie had also—rather astonishingly—adopted Solonik's orphaned son Emile, and—in an ironic turn of events— Emile was now fast-friends with Mary's Gemma, and Doyle's Edward. And this ironic turn of events was even stranger still, because Mary's Gemma was also adopted, and—like Emile—she was originally from Russia, so that Gemma and Emile could even speak in rudimentary Russian to each other.

So; Emile was the orphaned son of a notorious Russian criminal who'd been adopted by a notorious French criminal—an amazing turn of events, for certain—but Gemma's orphan-story was even more amazing than Emile's, if such a thing was possible. They'd discovered that Gemma was one of the last remaining remnants of the Russian royal family—that famous family who'd been killed in that famous revolution a long time ago.

As a small child, Gemma had been smuggled to England because her life had been at risk; the same political faction who'd brought about the revolution—so long ago—continued to hold a mighty grudge, and had murdered her parents. Luckily, an opposing faction had helped to hide Gemma—but not necessarily out of the kindness of their hearts; more so because the little girl could be made into a rallying point for their own cause.

And so, little Gemma had been stashed-away in London, but then the pertinent players who'd stashed her had all been killed in a turf-war, with the result that everyone lost track and even Mary thought the girl was only her first husband's daughter.

Fortunately, once Gemma's true identity had been discovered, the current Russian government—nervous, in their own right—had been all too happy to allow her to stay in London with her adopted family, and so all was well that ended well. Save for the sad fact that the girl's adopted father, Nigel Howard, had been unexpectedly killed, leaving Mary to fend on her own, along with Gemma and a brand-new baby daughter.

It had been a terrible tragedy, but Mary had plenty of support; aside from Lord and Lady Acton, Philippe Savoie had been an enormous help, and he'd shown himself to be a staunch supporter during Mary's difficult time. And—yet again—anyone else might be forgiven for thinking this behavior completely out-of-character save for Doyle. Doyle knew that—despite his hardened exterior—Savoie was a rescuer at heart.

Father John had once hinted that he thought Savoie's motives might be romantic, in helping-out the new widow, but Doyle didn't tend to agree with him; instead, she strongly suspected that Savoie's motive was to prevent Emile's best friend from moving away so as to go live with distant relatives. Savoie was an unrepentant bachelor, after all, and seemed to very much enjoy his criminal-kingpin way of life.

Mary's voice—rather hesitant—broke into Doyle's musings. "The prosecutor thought—he also suggested that I ask if you wouldn't mind attending the trial with me."

Caught by surprise, Doyle nonetheless hastened to assure her, "Of course I will, Mary; I was goin' to suggest that very thing."

This was a lie—such an idea had never entered Doyle's mind —but she could see why the request had been made. Doyle was a semi-famous figure around London, because she'd once rescued a colleague under death-defying circumstances. The press had played it up—the press loved it, when female police officers defied death—and now it was hard for her to go anywhere without someone recognizing her.

Unfortunately, Doyle held the certain conviction that the illustrious Chief Inspector would not like his wife to be used as a prop in a criminal trial, but it did make sense; it would be a prosecutorial boon, to have the heroic Officer Doyle throwing in her support at the murder trial.

"It keeps me up at nights, thinking about it," Mary confessed.

Doyle covered her companion's hand with her own. "Whist, Mary; we'll get through it, and Nigel would be so proud of you." Best not to mention that Nigel seemed more interested in scorched-earth vengeance than his poor wife's feelings—which was quite the surprise, all in all. He'd always been such a considerate husband, in life.

"Yes—you're right," Mary agreed with a show of resolution, and they turned to watch the two children again.

CHAPTER 6

*E*dward and Gemma were persuaded to pause for a moment so as to eat something, but the break was short-lived and they soon abandoned their sandwiches and raced off again toward the mounds of sand which were currently under construction.

"This is such a lovely place," Mary offered.

"It's old—it used to be some sort of smuggler's inn, back in the day. Acton likes to stay in places with a history." Doyle glanced up toward the house, to see that Mrs. Mackey was watching them from the bow-window. The woman smiled and waved, and Doyle and Mary waved back.

"She seems like a nice woman."

"I think she's local—she came with the house," Doyle explained. "Acton gave Trenton, Reynolds and Miss Valerie a holiday—I think he wanted as few movin' parts as possible."

"That was kind of him; it hasn't been an easy time for any of us."

Trust Mary, to be worried about the effect her husband's

murder had on everyone else. "To better days, Mary," Doyle offered.

"To better days," Mary agreed, and the two women toasted with their water bottles.

They sat in silence for a few minutes, idly watching the children. "Gemma's grown so tall," Doyle remarked.

"Yes, the pediatrician says her parents must have been tall. It's a shame that we'll probably never know anything about them."

"Are we absolutely certain they're no longer alive?" Doyle ventured.

Mary nodded. "Yes; the Russian authorities checked into it before they would allow us to adopt. They were killed, you know —Nigel said they should never have stayed in Russia. He said there are a lot of people there who still hate anything connected to the royal family."

Doyle shook her head slightly. "Imagine being so angry, and about somethin' that happened so long ago."

Mary—who never saw anything but the good in everyone, could only nod in agreement. "It *is* unbelievable—especially when they did nothing to deserve it."

Doyle noted, "It was lucky, in a strange way, that your Bill was given Gemma to hide so that she wound up with you, Mary."

"I know. I do think about it—about how different her life would have been, if she'd gone back. And we were so lucky that her adoption finally came through, even after Nigel was killed."

"There's the silver linin'," Doyle agreed, and privately thought it a much-welcome one; poor Mary's life had been brimful of hardships, but it would have broken the young woman in two to lose Gemma. "My own mum had her struggles, but we always had each other through thick and thin, and that made-up for everythin' else. You and Gemma are the same, I think."

With a conscious air, Mary ventured. "Although—although, I

could always marry again, I suppose. It's not as though I've soured on it."

Rather surprised that her companion had entertained such a thought, Doyle teased, "Third time's a charm."

Mary smiled. "It wouldn't be the same, of course. I'm older, and not so—well, a bit more practical, I suppose; not as many romantic notions as I used to have."

Doyle, who was living her own epic romance, protested, "You never know, Mary; another true love might be just 'round the corner. There's no rule that says you're only slated to have just the one."

To her surprise, the other woman looked away, and Doyle caught a fleeting sense of consciousness that was very unusual for gentle Mary. "Yes. Well, along those lines—I wanted to tell you—I wanted to confess that I've done something—I've done something a little foolish."

With an indulgent smile, Doyle teased, "Have you? Then you must tell me all about it, here and now."

"Yes. Well, I—I suppose you could say I was—I was inappropriate, with Philippe Savoie."

Doyle stared at her, agog.

Seeing her reaction, Mary raised her hands to her flushed cheeks and retreated. "Oh; oh, please don't think—"

But—with a massive effort—Doyle recovered her wits and said lightly, "Faith, Mary; who can blame you? That girl who runs the kiosk at the park nearly faints, every time he speaks to her."

"I know," said Mary, with an air of impatience. "She's a bit silly, to think that he'd be interested."

There was a small silence, and then Doyle ventured, "Can you tell me? If you'd rather not, just say it's none o' my business and we'll speak of it no more."

Mary met her eyes. "You won't tell anyone?"

"My hand on my heart," Doyle assured her, because she'd the strong impression that the other woman was longing for a confidante. Not to mention that Doyle was that gob-smacked, wondering how such an extraordinary event had come about.

Her cheeks still pink, Mary began, "He came over the other morning to go over the accounts—he likes to keep track, every month, since I'm not very good at such things. He offered to make tea, and went into the kitchen, but then he burned his finger when he was fiddling with the stove. I brought him some ice in a dishtowel, and then—and then—"

Since Mary seemed stuck, Doyle prompted, "He kissed you?"

Wide-eyed, the other woman nodded. "Yes—yes. And then I *threw* myself at him; it was as though—as though I'd taken complete leave of my *senses*."

"Faith; I know *that* feeling," Doyle pronounced, with some fervor.

Earnestly, Mary replied, "Yes—I thought you might understand. I was just—I guess I was just desperate to feel—to feel that *weight* again." Pausing, she shook her head slightly in wonder. "You don't realize how much you miss it."

"That, you don't," Doyle heartily agreed.

There was a small silence. "I'll have to go to Confession, I suppose."

"Either way, there's no fault to you, Mary," Doyle advised, and congratulated herself for sounding so matter-of-fact, when she was *truly* having trouble keeping her mouth from falling open. "We're only human, after all."

"That's what he said—Philippe. Afterward, I was so embarrassed—I could hardly look at him. But he—he was so kind, and said something about how it only meant that I was coming alive again, and that I shouldn't feel ashamed."

"He has the right of it; you shouldn't," Doyle said stoutly.

"I don't know—I don't think I can bring myself to tell Father John that the baby was asleep in the next room."

"As long as you didn't wake her, she's not goin' to judge you, Mary."

The other woman chuckled, and Doyle chuckled in turn. They then sat together for a moment whilst Doyle tried to think of what she should say.

"I suppose the French take a different view," Mary offered.

"I think it's men, who take a different view, and it doesn't much matter where they come from," Doyle declared, and both women chuckled yet again.

But Mary was not yet finished with her story. "He told me if I was pregnant, we'd go tell Father John, and get married."

Doyle stared at her, astonished all over again. "*Savoie* said that?"

"Yes. It hadn't even occurred to me, Lady Acton—which only shows you how—how *crazed*, I was."

"D'you think you're pregnant?" Doyle ventured.

"No—I don't think so. And I'm still breastfeeding, after all."

Doyle nodded. "So; was it a one-off, d'you think? Can you carry on as though nothin' happened?"

"No," Mary replied honestly. "But I have to try. I can't make things awkward, and it's not as though I'm a teenager."

"That girl in the kiosk would turn green with envy," Doyle observed, and Mary laughed aloud.

CHAPTER 7

They'd returned from the beach, and after Doyle put-down Edward for his nap—he was exhausted, and for once didn't protest—she took the first opportunity she could to ring-up her husband.

"Kathleen," he said. "How was your outing?"

"Never mind that," she said impatiently. "We've a Code-One, husband; my hormones have sorted themselves out and I'm longin' to feel your weight."

Her husband was understandably surprised by this unexpected request. "Is that so? We do have house guests."

"Well, think of somethin' whilst the boys are asleep—is it too undignified to sneak off to have sex in the car?"

"Probably; it's in an open carport."

"Oh—oh, that's right."

He offered, "There is an underground passage, in the cellar."

Doyle blinked in surprise. "There is?"

"Yes. It's been there since the place was an inn for smugglers. The passageway goes from the cellar to the beach."

She smiled into the phone. "Is there a secret panel? I'll not bite, unless there's a secret panel."

"A secret door, more accurately."

"Sold," she declared. "I'll be sneakin' off in two shakes."

"Give me ten minutes, and I will meet you there."

With a conscious air, Doyle crept downstairs—she could hear Mary speaking with Gemma as she fed baby Hannah in her room —and tried to decide how best to avoid Mrs. Mackey, so as to make her way down the cellar stairs from the kitchen. This turned out to be no problem, as the housekeeper was mounting the steps herself, and heading toward Mary's door with a tea-tray.

Doyle smiled, as she stood aside. "I won't be needin' a tray, Mrs. Mackey."

"Oh—oh, very well, Lady Acton."

Well, that puts me in my place, Doyle thought in amusement, as she continued down the steps. Mrs. Mackey hadn't even thought to fetch me a tea-tray, which only goes to show that everyone recognizes that Mary is quality, and never mind who has the stupid titles pinned onto their names.

The house was quiet, and Doyle slipped through the cellar door, pausing for a moment to allow her eyes to adjust to the dimness. She descended the stairs carefully—the place was old, and therefore the steps were narrow—with only a bare light bulb for illumination. Once she came to the cellar floor, she began to walk with her hand running lightly along the wall, looking for the secret door.

It wasn't so very secret, after all; there it was, looking rather like an ordinary pantry door embedded in the stone wall. She lifted the latch and pulled, and the door opened rather easily, the hinges well-oiled.

I've a good guess, now, as to where my husband goes off to

wander at night, Doyle thought; and it well-suits him—he's not one to want anyone else to notice when he comes and goes.

The tunnel was narrow and hewn out of rock, so it was cool, and smelt of the sea—even as it was a bit musty. Doyle closed the door behind her and stood for a moment in its confines, the sand soft beneath her feet and the echoes of the past reverberating from the walls.

I hope Acton comes soon, she thought; I don't much like hanging about, in echoing old places.

She was to have her wish, because the door behind her opened and then the figure of her husband stood silhouetted in relief for a moment, before he closed it behind him. With a pang, she realized that he'd lost a bit of weight—and shame on her, for not having noticed. He's been fretting himself to pieces about something, she thought, and I'd best get crackin' and find out what it is, before he wears himself down to a thread.

Therefore, she didn't hesitate to walk into his arms as he brought his mouth down to hers. With some impatience, she pulled at his shirt but he broke away for a moment, murmuring, "Allow me to put the blanket down."

"Mmm," she responded, and began pulling at his belt with her free hand.

"Hold still—just for a moment, Kathleen."

"No," she said breathlessly, and ran her eager hands under his shirt—faith, but he was a fine specimen of a man—skinny or no.

He gave up—always one to take the hint, was Acton—and he allowed her to pull him down to the sand, the heat between them igniting in a rush, and his body as familiar as her own.

Now, this was a good idea, she thought, as she impatiently pressed herself against his long length. God bless Mary, for giving me the inspiration—although I should probably include Savoie, too, since no doubt he was the instigator, despite what Mary might think.

Hastily deciding that the last needful thing was for her husband to discover that Philippe Savoie had inspired her to go sex-mad, Doyle instead happily surrendered to the pleasures of the flesh—which were truly amazing, and had been very much missed.

After a satisfying round of sneaking-off sex—which was surely the best kind—she lay beside him on their backs in the sand, as he idly held her hand aloft and traced its outlines with his fingers.

With the subject so close to mind, Doyle debated whether to tell her husband of Mary's little lapse—faith, this was juicy gossip and he'd never say anything; Acton was a champion keeper-of-secrets—but something held her back. She knew that her husband wouldn't be best pleased, that Mary had thrown caution to the winds with Philippe Savoie; he was annoyed with Savoie, just now. They'd had a bit of drama, recently, and even though Acton never made mention of the Frenchman, Doyle knew—in the way that she knew things—that her husband wasn't happy with the man. She'd a strong feeling that this latest news about Mary wouldn't do anything to lessen that annoyance, and so it would probably be best to say nothing.

Besides, it seemed likely that Acton was slated to find out anyway, and sooner rather than later. Mary wasn't the type to dally 'neath the hedgerows, and—despite what Doyle had said about men—Savoie was very much a man in control of himself. He wouldn't have participated unless he was willing to commit. Rather like the man who lay beside her, as a matter of fact.

With a fond smile, she asked, "D'you remember that first time you kissed me, at the crime scene?"

"I'll not soon forget. Although I think it was you who kissed me, more accurately."

"Aye, and I make no excuses. Faith, but I was yearnin'."

"So was I."

"Well, you hid it better. You were that good, at keepin' yourself to yourself back in the day." She paused. "Not so much, now; I'm much wiser to your ways, husband."

He didn't respond, but continued to idly trace her fingers.

So; he wasn't going to budge, which was very much in keeping. Therefore, she decided to take a more direct approach. "You've been a bit pulled-about, lately."

"Yes," he agreed. "I am sorry, Kathleen."

"Whist; don't apologize—I only wish I could help. Is it Tommy? I could try to give him back."

She could sense his smile. "Tommy is a delight."

"He's always watchin' Edward like a jackdaw watches a shiny hairpin."

"Is that a good thing, or a bad thing?"

"Depends on whether you enjoy bein' run ragged. And speakin' of such, d'you need more time to yourself, mayhap? Would that help?" This was a shrewd guess; Acton was—at heart —a solitary soul, and for good reason.

He brought her hand down to hold it against his chest, and she could feel him take a long breath. "No," he replied. "I need less time to myself."

With some sympathy, she squeezed the hand that held hers. "Let me take a crack at it. You're that frustrated about somethin'— I think it has to do with how the Public Accounts case landed— and you're not one who bears bein' frustrated very well. D'you think we can skip over the hard part—where I spend a lot of time and effort bird-doggin' the truth—and instead jump ahead to the part where you straight-out tell me who's got herself burnt-up?"

Slowly, he revealed, "I was called-in, because a prominent actress has gone missing, and the victim may indeed be she."

This was a wrinkle, and Doyle blinked in surprise. "Oh? I thought there was a Public Accounts connection."

"The two things are not mutually exclusive."

He was carefully choosing his words, and with some impatience, she scolded, "You're makin' me bird-dog, here, husband."

Thus prompted, he explained, "The missing actress is Russian, and there have long been rumors that her ex-husband is connected to the Russian mafia."

With a frown, Doyle asked in confusion, "The Russian *mafia* was involved in the Public Accounts rig?"

"To an extent."

Again, he was choosing his words, and suddenly, the penny dropped; Savoie and his Russian counterpart, Solonik, had set-up the original smuggling-rig here in England, but when Solonik landed in prison, Acton had stepped-in to team up with Savoie in his place. Or at least, that was what Doyle had pieced together— Acton was as close as a sphynx when it came to his questionable enterprises.

So; it was probably best not to delve into the particulars of Solonik's downfall, and instead Doyle offered, "I suppose the Russians are due to cause trouble; they've been layin' low, ever since the turf-wars, and now they're probably feelin' their oats again—not to mention missin' their loot. Why would they kill this actress, though? Was she turnin' state's evidence against them, or somethin'?"

"Very unlikely. She was an active member of the Mossovet."

There was a small silence. Honestly, thought Doyle, as she held on to her patience with both hands; it's like pulling *teeth*. "And what's that, my friend?"

"A rather radical political group, which tends to promote socialist causes and disparage the sitting government. She was heavily involved in the group's fund-raising, due to her status, but then she stepped back approximately three years ago."

"She saw the light, and decided to become a monarchist?" Doyle joked.

"Unlikely. But there was good reason to take a lower profile. Her political activities tended to bring unwanted scrutiny for her husband."

She could only see the sense in this. "If he's mafia, he'd hate anything that brought attention."

"One could presume. Nevertheless they divorced, with allegations of infidelity on both sides."

Doyle made a face. "Not a surprise I suppose, if she's a famous actress, and he's a wealthy kingpin."

"Indeed."

Doyle thought this over. "The manner of her death looks to be sendin' a nasty message."

"I would agree," he replied.

"Could we be watchin' another turf-war, startin' to unfold? Mayhap a rival group killed her as a warnin' to the Russians to mind their own business?"

"It is possible. Although she is rather high-profile for an admonishment-murder."

This was true; as a practical matter, rival gangs—and the Russian mafia in particular—didn't like to draw attention to themselves whilst sending out a message to their rivals. If the victim was indeed this famous actress, it tended to weigh against hers being an admonishment-murder, since the rival groups wouldn't much like all the publicity surrounding her death.

"If she's havin' affairs, mayhap it was a wronged wife that killed her," Doyle suggested. "We shouldn't overlook the obvious, I suppose."

"Quite possible."

She turned her head toward him. "But you don't think so."

"It was a professional job, with little evidence left behind."

She amended, "A wronged wife who could afford a good hit-man."

"Possibly."

Doyle finally decided that patience was over-rated, and so she straight-out accused, "There's somethin' here, that you're not tellin' me, Michael. Please don't fob me off, else I'll be hirin' a hit-man myself."

His chest rose and fell. "Sir Vikili was present at the morgue, today."

Doyle turned her head to stare at him in surprise; Sir Vikili was a renowned criminal defense solicitor who tended to represent only the very wealthiest of villains. "Now, that's a bit odd; dead people don't need solicitors."

"I would agree."

"Who's he's protectin', then? Whoever killed her?"

"Perhaps. But it appears there are some very cautious people who are interested in monitoring our investigation."

With a frown, Doyle turned her head so as to regard the rock-hewn ceiling again. "Aye, that. Cautious people who are able to afford Sir Vikili—which is a mighty small universe. He's done some Russian mafia, before—didn't he represent Solonik? Leave it to him, to help these villains wriggle off the hook."

"This victim is not doing much wriggling."

She smiled, slightly. "Now, there's some fine gallows humor. Mayhap the Russian mafia did have her killed—she double-crossed them or somethin'—and now they're sendin' in Sir Vikili so as to cover their tracks."

"I would be surprised; ever since her divorce, she seems to have stepped away from controversy. And I caught the sense that

Sir Vikili was attempting to make an identification, also. So; whoever sent him is not certain that the victim is indeed she."

"Faith, that's all very interestin'. When will you have an ID?"

"There were bone fragments, so DNA will be sought. We will compare dental records today—it looks as though there were ceramic veneers on most of the teeth."

"It does sound like this actress, then."

She debated whether or not to press him, because she could sense that he was holding his cards close to the vest, for some reason—not to mention that he'd a history of switching-out burnt-up corpses to suit his own needs. "I will—yet again—skip over the tedious part, and ask you to tell me straight-out that this was not your doin', husband."

"No," he replied immediately, as though he'd been expecting the question. "Neither the fire nor the homicide."

CHAPTER 8

*I*t was the truth, and she'd rather expected it because—whilst he was definitely unhappy about something—it didn't seem to fit the usual situation where Acton was behaving badly. It was a sad testament that there was a "usual situation" in the first place, but there it was; when Acton was in the process of imposing his own notions of justice on some hapless soul, he tended to fall into a fearsome black mood, rather than this strange and protracted brooding-spell. So; he wasn't behind this latest crime, but he knew more than he was letting on, which meant that it was business-as-usual with respect to the fair Doyle's foray into marriage.

"I'm going to find out whatever-it-is," she warned. "I always do."

"Perhaps it would not be for the best, Kathleen."

The words hung in the air for a moment, and then she replied in an exasperated tone, "What you might think is 'best' and what I might think is 'best' aren't always the same thing, Michael. I say let the chips fall where they may; everythin' only gets miles worse when you try to manipulate the outcome—a lesson learned, and learned fairly recently, I might add."

"All too true," he replied, in a mild tone.

Oh-oh, she thought, and abruptly changed her tactics—chiding herself for making a tactical mistake; no point in ruining the progress she'd made in softening him up by pointing out the wages of sin. The last needful thing was to set-up his defenses so that he retreated from her, and went back to brooding on the moors and plotting dark doings.

Therefore, she offered in a lighter tone, "And leave it to you, to find a house with a secret tunnel, custom-made for skulkin' about. Next, you'll be buildin' a tunnel at Trestles."

"I am not sure where it would lead," he pointed out reasonably.

"Where there's a will, there's a way, my friend. How old's this one?"

"Dating back to Napoleonic times, at least. Smuggling has always been prevalent, in this area."

Thoughtfully, Doyle eyed the rocky ceiling above them. "I think it was spies, along with the smugglers. The Home Office had to keep a close eye on the coast, back then."

There was a small pause. "I won't ask how you would know such a thing."

"Best not," she teased. "It would make your hair stand on end."

But she was distracted, because her scalp had started prickling, the way it did when her perceptive abilities were telling her to pay attention. What? Was someone a spy?

She closed her eyes for a moment, trying to grasp at the elusive thought, but came up empty. Just as well; the last needful thing was to be pitched into a Home Office spy-ring caper—she'd enough on her plate already.

"Did you enjoy our holiday?"

"It was lovely, truly," she said diplomatically. "But I'm that tired of lollin'-about."

He lifted her hand to kiss it. "I wouldn't call it lolling-about. You have been very busy."

"Whist, I just needed to get the hang of handlin' two at a time. And peacefulness is nice in small doses, Michael, but I think I've had my fill. Besides, you're needed at home, to delve into this poor veneered actress's death."

"Yes. It may be necessary to re-assemble the task force from the Public Accounts case."

She raised her brows. "Oh-ho; Sir Vikili has you that spooked, then?"

"It would pay to be cautious, certainly."

"Well—on the bright side—mayhap a lead will turn up so that we can finally chase-down Charbonneau. She's one who's managed to slip the net."

He replied, "I think we can safely assume that Ms. Charbonneau is no longer alive."

This was of interest, since Acton usually knew of which he spoke. "A containment-murder, to keep her from talkin'?"

"I would imagine."

"Well, if she's been silenced, Michael, that goes back to my original theory that there's someone else out there—a major player who's also slipped the net."

"Perhaps."

She made a wry mouth, because he was being careful to couch his words so that she couldn't spot the lie; little did he know, that she'd a handy ghost who was bringing up this very subject. Nigel Howard seemed to think that they'd got hold of the wrong leg, somehow, and now—now she'd the strong sense that Acton was aware of this same thing; he knew who'd escaped the mills of justice in the Public Accounts case. Mayhap that was what was giving him fits, and making him walk the moors, a'nights. It was all very strange; after all, Acton was rarely stymied when it came to knocking heads together.

She rubbed her hand gently on his chest. "Somethin's bitin' at you, my friend. Can't you tell me?"

"It is nothing that I cannot resolve, Kathleen—please don't worry."

The words were said in a dismissive tone, but she persisted, "I'm that good at gettin' you untangled, husband."

His chest rose and fell. "You are, indeed. Forgive me for being so short with you."

She nestled her head against his shoulder, and he willingly drew her close to his side. She offered, "Whenever anyone in the class was nursin' a grievance, Sister Luke would give us a lecture about the Wells of Isaac—if I've heard it once, I've heard it a *million* times."

"What would she say?"

"Isaac was lookin' for a new place to move his people—they had flocks of sheep, and such, back in Bible times. Two times he found a good place, and went to a lot of trouble to dig wells so as to make it work, but each time the locals would move-in after he'd done all the work, and claim it for themselves. So, rather than fight them about it, he just kept movin' on, and on the third time he came to a place that was miles better than all the ones he'd given up." She paused. "I think the lesson is, it's not worth the quarrel, and peace is its own reward."

He considered this silently for a moment. "I think I prefer the story of King David at Ziklag."

"Oh-oh," she said in alarm; "I suppose that's in keepin'—he wiped everyone out, didn't he?"

"Justly deserved."

"You do like a good vengeance-story," she conceded.

He turned to take her into his arms, and pull her against him—ready to have another go, he was. "On the other hand, King David had many wives, and I am content with just the one."

She smiled. "An archwife, who hounds you without pause."

"You hounded me into this tunnel, certainly."

She giggled. "I should dress-up as a pirate wench—I finally have the bosom for it."

He ran his hand over her hip. "I prefer this outfit."

"Best hurry along—we should probably sneak back, soon. Everyone's goin' to wonder where we went."

He began to nuzzle her neck. "Let them."

She sighed, and moved her head so as to grant him greater access. "Aye, aye, sir."

CHAPTER 9

$\mathcal{I}$t was the following day, and Doyle and Mary had taken the two older children to the beach again whilst the smaller children took their morning nap. It wasn't as sunny today, and so they were huddled in their fleece jackets and sitting on the blanket, as Gemma and Edward added to the ruins of yesterday's sandcastle. As was the case with such visits, all pressing topics of conversation had been exhausted on the first day, and so the two young women now just sat together, comfortably silent.

"Gemma is loving this visit," Mary offered. "And Mrs. Mackey is helping her sort her collection of shells, to choose the ones to bring home for art projects—she's been so helpful. Has Callie been for a visit?"

"No—I think Acton didn't want many visitors," Doyle replied in a mild tone, even as it had now become clear to her why this was; something was afoot, and Acton wanted to keep all curious sets of eyes to a minimum.

"How is Callie?" Mary asked, a bit tentatively.

"She seems to be doin' better," Doyle replied. "Fingers crossed."

Callie was Acton's younger half-sister, who'd discovered this unexpected fact rather abruptly, poor thing. Lately, Callie had been assisting with nannying-duties whilst Mary was weathering her bereavement, and Doyle held the suspicion that Acton was feeling rather impatient with the younger girl. Doyle could sympathize with poor Callie though; it couldn't be easy, to discover that one's identity was not at all what one had assumed, and—after all—Callie was young and still finding her feet.

And it didn't help matters that Callie's birth-mother, Melinda, was practically smothering the girl with long-suppressed maternal love. Melinda was an aristocrat— originally from Acton's neighborhood—and was not one to temper her actions or even understand the need to.

Reminded, Doyle added, "Poor Melinda's a bit beset; her late husband's mother is suspicious that Melinda murdered him. She's even hired investigators."

Utterly shocked, Mary stared at her. "Oh, *poor* Melinda! What a *terrible* thing to think."

Doyle had to smile. "You'd never make a detective, Mary. You're not half cynical enough."

Surprised, Mary ventured, "You don't *really* think that Melinda would kill her husband?"

"Well, he was supposed to be an RC priest, after all, and they were married for all of five minutes before she inherited a ton of money. You can see why his mother might be suspicious—not to mention that you learn fairly quickly, in our business, that anyone is capable of anythin'."

"Not Melinda," Mary insisted. "She hasn't the energy."

Doyle laughed. "Now, there's a thought. Mayhap you'd make a good detective after all. I'll see if the CID has any openings."

Mary bent her head, as she smoothed the sand with an idle hand. "I may go back to nannying, actually. I feel as though I should make a push to support myself—or at least contribute. I know I can't afford Gemma's school—and bless you for that, Lady Acton—but I should try to get back on my own feet, after the year's end."

This was unexpected, and Doyle raised her brows. "Well, if that's what you decide to do, you will nanny for no one save us, Mary. Callie can be your assistant, because we've plenty of children, and Acton's got plenty of money."

A bit doubtfully, Mary asked, "But what of your new nanny?"

"Miss Valerie's out the door in a pig's whisker," Doyle declared. "She's passin' fair, but she can't hold a candle to you."

"Oh—" said Mary, rather distressed; "Oh, I didn't mean to suggest—"

But Doyle only shrugged in unconcern, mainly because she was fairly certain that Mary was protesting a little too much; she must be aware, on some level, that Savoie was behaving like a man on a mission, and therefore the chances were slim that she'd actually be called upon to support herself any time soon. "Acton likes the new nanny because she's very precise and organized— the same as he is. I'm at the other end of the spectrum, and so she makes me a bit nervous—I think she reminds me of the Mother Superior at St. Brigid's; I'm half expectin' her to tell me to stand-up straight."

Mary laughed. "How does Edward like her?"

Doyle quirked her mouth. "Edward's testin' her mettle, of course, and it's a close-run thing as to who will prevail."

Smiling fondly in the direction of the two children, Mary offered, "He is such a dear little boy."

Doyle laughed aloud. "He's the King of the Rascals, Mary, and he's got you wound 'round his finger."

They sat for a few minutes in companionable silence, and then Mary asked, "We're close to Bristol, aren't we?"

"Aye—it's just up the coast. I've never been; Acton wanted to stay here instead, because he thinks Bristol is too crowded." Best not to mention that a secret tunnel seemed to factor heavily into the decision.

"I think Philippe was headed to Bristol, yesterday—I'm fairly certain that's what he told me. He has business there, and he said he had to go check-up on things. One of his properties caught fire, and he had to go inspect the damage."

Doyle stilled, as she stared at the waves.

"I really don't know much about his business," Mary continued, and then rather hurriedly added, "Not that it's any of my own business, of course."

But Doyle didn't reply, because she was still trying to assimilate this rather alarming revelation. Did the burnt yachts indeed belong to Savoie? That seemed unlikely, because—if the yachts were involved somehow in the Public Accounts case—the last thing a decent criminal would do, would be to have his name printed plainly on the title. And surely—if that were the case— Acton would have made mention? Although, she did have the sense that Acton and Savoie weren't getting along, lately.

With a knit brow, she considered this. Acton had said he wasn't the one who'd burnt the yachts—and it was the truth—but could it have been Savoie? Could Savoie be destroying evidence that might implicate his role in the Public Accounts case?

On its face, this might seem a semi-plausible theory, save for the fact that there hadn't been the slightest whisper of a hint that Savoie was a suspect in the Public Accounts case. In fact, Acton would make certain of that, because if Savoie became a suspect that would open-up a trail of evidence that led straight to Acton.

So; it seemed very unlikely that Savoie was the one burning

the yachts. But—lest she forget—Sir Vikili had represented Savoie, in the past, and it would certainly explain the solicitor's unexpected appearance at the morgue; he would want to make certain that no one was nosing around his notorious client, and fingering him as a suspect.

Which was—again—a semi-plausible theory, save for the fact that Acton was no fool, and would have guessed the same thing. Instead, she'd the sense that Acton was genuinely puzzled—and rather wary—about Sir Vikili's little visit to the Bristol morgue. Worried enough to think he might have missed something, and re-open the Pubic Accounts task force.

It all seemed a bit ominous, and—after deciding that she'd best find out if Mary could shed some light—Doyle ventured, "It was some fancy yachts that caught fire, wasn't it? I'd heard from Mrs. Mackey that there was a fire at the Marina a few nights back."

But Mary shook her head. "No; Philippe said it was a coin shop—you know, one of those places where the collectors go to buy coins."

Doyle stared at her. Worse and worse, she thought. The Bristol coin shop had been another cog in the smuggling machine—coin shops were notorious for fencing goods and for laundering money. And now—now, it seemed that both the yachts and the shop had been permanently removed from any-and-all smuggling operations, courtesy of a hearty helping of arson. Not to mention there was a dead actress who was connected to the Russian mafia —and not to mention that Doyle's husband was brooding, and that a vengeful ghost had shown-up to haunt her dreams. Something massive was brewing, and she'd best shake her stumps and find out what-was-what.

This seemed a daunting task, for someone on maternity leave, but there was no time to spare; Acton had the bit between his teeth, and she'd the sense he was that angry—at Savoie, mayhap?

Which only served to remind her that if Mary was thinking of casting-in her lot with the likes of Philippe Savoie, it would be like pairing-up a lamb with a wolf and the fair Doyle should probably make a push to give her the head's up.

Therefore, whilst Doyle considered how to casually bring up the fact that Savoie wasn't a businessman so much as he was a criminal kingpin with an occurrence-sheet as long as your arm, Mary's voice broke into her thoughts.

"There's Mrs. Mackey." She waved at the housekeeper, who was watching them again from the bow window.

Doyle waved also, and remarked, "Another Mother Superior, Mary. She probably thinks we're daft, to have the children out here in the cold."

"Oh, no—she's very sweet," Mary protested. "And she's been so helpful with the girls—even though she's supposed to be helping you with your boys. I feel a bit guilty."

"She likes yours better," Doyle teased. "I can't blame her."

Mary laughed. "She mentioned that she was coming to London on holiday, and I invited her to stay with us if she'd like. She said she'd be staying with one of her children, instead, but she promised she'd come by for a visit."

"That's kind of you, Mary—you've your hands full." Leave it to Mary, to take-on out-of-town guests whilst her husband's murder case was going forward.

But Mary only admitted, "It's no hardship—she's so helpful. She says Gemma reminds her of her own Jamie, when she was little."

Well, that's funny, Doyle thought; I could have sworn that she said her Jamie was a boy.

CHAPTER 10

A few days after Mary left for home, they packed-up to return home themselves, which was somewhat of a relief to Doyle. She needed to be in back in London in order to do whatever digging that she could, and mayhap Acton wouldn't be as wound-up if he was back at the Met, task-forcing or doing whatever else was needed so as to soothe his spirit. That his spirit needed soothing seemed clear; he continued to walk, late at night, and she'd the sense he was making a massive effort to hide his distraction—and its cause—from the wife of his bosom.

Plotting, she thought with some resignation; he was plotting—she knew the signs. Plotting and fretting, in equal parts. Katy bar the door, because whatever-it-was, it was a corker.

And so, Doyle was not at all surprised when the ghost of Nigel Howard showed up that last night, and she rather wished she could make a better report.

"I'm not doin' so well, with this avengin' business," she immediately confessed. "I'm a bit hampered, by bein' here, instead of in town."

The ghost smiled at her in a manner that offered gentle encouragement. "Keep at it; you're making good progress."

She blinked. "But—I haven't done anythin' yet."

"You mustn't worry—you'll get there."

"Acton's worryin' enough for the both of us—I think he knows whatever-it-is that you're tryin' to tell me."

"No, he doesn't," the ghost corrected her, almost kindly.

Doyle stared at him in confusion. "No? Mayhap it would be helpful, then, if you would give me a tiny little hint."

Almost apologetically, the ghost explained, "It's all rather complicated, I'm afraid. There are ancient alliances, and ancient grudges."

"There *always* are," she groused. "And it's what leads to a lot of our homicide cases—*why* can't everyone just move on?"

He nodded. "An old lament—it stems right from the very beginning."

But she reminded him, "Not necessarily; Isaac moved on, and he's from Genesis—which is as 'beginning' as it gets. No vengeance or wrath for him."

"Not quite that far back, perhaps," the ghost amended.

"King David didn't move on," Doyle admitted. "Talk about vengeance—he takes the palm."

"If you would avenge me," the ghost suggested, "I would appreciate it."

Again, Doyle was struck by the—by the *strangeness* of this; that Nigel Howard's kind exterior hid the burning heart of a vengeance-seeker—although a burning heart was perhaps not the best way of putting it, since the man was dead. "I'll do my best," she hedged. "I think I'm more of an Isaac than a David."

He was silent, hovering without comment, and so she offered, "Mary was here with the girls; I don't know if you know."

The ghost smiled fondly. "She's a marvelous baker, you know.

I've always been very fond of her bread-pudding. She uses red currants for flavor—simply delightful."

This seemed a bit off-topic—considering that the topic was Biblical wrath—and Doyle ventured, "I thought you were the healthy-eatin' type, like Acton is."

"Bread-pudding was always my fatal weakness," he confessed. "I was quite fond. As is Hector."

Be patient, Doyle reminded herself; he wouldn't be here and saying these nonsensical things without good reason. "Who's this, now?"

"My watch-dog," he explained, and brought his benign gaze back to her.

"Oh, that's right," said Doyle, doing her best to keep up. "You had a dog."

The ghost smiled. "Hector is a good fellow—even though he's been known to bite. Very loyal—and rather ferocious, when necessary. The best kind of watch-dog."

Doyle admitted, "Dogs don't like me, much."

"This one does."

Doyle decided not to point out to the ghost that she'd never met his dog—they were already wandering off-topic—and so instead, she told him, "She's doin' well, I think—Mary is. She was knocked off her pins, but now she's righted herself."

"Her ways are the ways of gentleness, and all her paths are peace."

"That's our Mary," Doyle agreed. "She's a walkin' angel." Best not mention that she'd engaged in a round of raging-sex with Philippe Savoie; even a walking angel deserved a bit of leeway. Not to mention that her dead husband seemed a little too bent on vengeance, so the two of them were even, in a way.

The ghost continued, "You saved me, once; now you must save my poor Mary."

Doyle blinked in surprise. "Save *Mary*? Save her from what?"

But she'd awakened to the empty bed beside her, and the echoing sound of the waves against the shore.

CHAPTER 11

*D*oyle used the car-ride the next day to ponder the ghost's message—such as it was; you'd think someone who'd been an MP could manage to be a little clearer, and it probably came from having to talk in circles all the time. But somewhere—in that scattering of unrelated topics—there was something important, and it would be miles easier if he'd have just stuck to the script.

Unfortunately, the car rides were no longer the haven of peace they used to be, since Edward took the opportunity to make faces at Tommy, who nearly passed out from wheezing baby-laughter every time he did. Finally, the vibrations and the droning noise worked their magic and the two boys nodded off the sleep, leaving Doyle with a few minutes of blessed silence to contemplate the passing scenery.

The most alarming thing about the ghostly conversation, she decided, was that Howard seemed to think that Mary was in some kind of danger. This was rather shocking, since it was so unexpected; if Howard had been targeted because of his work on the Public Accounts case, there should be no reason for the villains to go after his wife—especially now that the scheme had been rolled-up. Although it did seem clear that someone must have slipped the net; Howard was calling for revenge, and Acton was being all tight-lipped and grim about something. And that actress had been killed—if she was connected, somehow, it did seem as though the case had not yet been put to bed, despite the upcoming trial.

Aloud, she asked thoughtfully, "Tell me more about this Russian actress, Michael. What do we know about her?"

"Sasha Lanska. She had a long career in the theatre—no films, or anything commercial; she considered herself a serious artist. Because she tended to be politically outspoken, the press loved to seek her opinion."

Doyle nodded, having paid no attention whatsoever to West End theatre goings-on, which may as well have taken place on Mars. "Had she been spotted at the Marina before?"

"Dockworkers say no." He paused. "However, the dockworkers seem very reticent."

Doyle took a guess at what "reticent" meant, and replied thoughtfully, "You can hardly blame them, Michael—people are gettin' themselves burnt-up. Did you have a chance to flash your badge and bully them a bit?"

"I did. I was not as impressive as I'd hoped."

She smiled, slightly. "You should have brought me along to listen to what they had to say, Michael."

"A good point. Perhaps I still will."

She turned to gaze out the window again, because—despite his equivocal words—she knew that he didn't want her anywhere near this. It seemed clear that he was worried she would discover something he didn't want her to, and—for once —it didn't seem to be a situation where she was investigating a flippin' murder that her flippin' husband had committed himself —which was certainly an improvement and thank God fastin'. But nonetheless, there was something here that he didn't want her to know. Howard's ghost knew whatever-it-was, but he couldn't seem to stop talking in circles about random and unrelated topics.

Reminded, Doyle turned to her husband again. "Didn't Nigel Howard have a dog? Whatever happened to it? I don't remember ever seein' a dog at their flat."

Her husband raised his brows, but ably managed to keep up with this unexpected change of subject. "The dog died sometime back, I believe. It may have been before they were married."

Doyle knit her brow, trying to make sense of the ghost's comments. "Did Howard ever bring him over to our flat?"

"No—he tended to keep him well-away from strangers. A mastiff, with an uncertain temper. Raven was his name."

Doyle turned to stare at him. "The dog's name was *Raven*? Are you sure?" Faith, she was certain that Howard had called him Hector—hadn't he?

"I believe so." He couldn't help but smile. "Why the sudden interest? Do you think Edward needs a dog?"

She reminded him in a repressive tone, "Dogs don't like me much, Michael."

"Right," he said, in the tone of one who knows this and thus is not certain why the subject has come up.

"I was just thinkin' about it, is all."

After deciding that she'd best get back to the topic at hand, she continued, "But about this actress; if I were guessin', I'd guess that hers was an admonishment-murder with a dash of arson thrown in, just so as to emphasize the fact. So; despite her divorce, she must have been meddlin' with the wrong people, Michael. Mayhap she wanted to tweak her ex-husband by cozyin' up to his rivals." She glanced over at him. "Does the ex-husband have any rivals who might be likely suspects?"

"Her husband was Igor Denisovich, who was a known-associate with Solonik, and Barayev. All three men originated from St. Petersburg."

"Mother a' Mercy," she exclaimed in surprise. "We *are* goin' back to the very beginnin'." Solonik and Barayev were two players who'd met a bad end, some time ago; Solonik was the one who'd been double-crossing Philippe Savoie, and Barayev—Solonik's brother-in-law—had crossed Acton, which was oftentimes equally as fatal, unfortunately.

Understandably confused, her husband tilted his head toward her. "What's that?"

Slowly, she explained, "It just seems so strange—that none of this is ever over and done with. These same characters keep poppin' up—like a jack o' the clock—even after they're long dead."

But he only offered, "It is the nature of a turf-war, unfortunately. The groups are still pitted against each other, even though the individual players may come and go."

"Ancient grudges," she said slowly, quoting the ghost. "And ancient allegiances."

"Indeed. As we have often seen."

Right, then; she thought—somewhat relieved to see a glimmer of sense in Howard's mish-mash of topics. He'd told her that she needed to go back to the beginning, and that there were ancient grudges—which seemed to tie-in very nicely with this actress-death, and the Russian mafia angle.

Thoughtfully, she suggested, "It sounds as though we should go and take a gander at this mafia ex-husband."

"Yes. As soon as we have a solid ID."

She nodded, and idly looked through the windscreen,

contemplating the fact that her guileful husband seemed to have no objection to the fair Doyle being exposed to whatever the victim's ex-husband would have to say, even as whatever the dockworkers might tell her was another matter altogether. Which would lead one to the conclusion that the mafia-husband would tell them nothing of interest.

Reminded, she asked, "Who owned the yachts?"

"A limited company."

Doyle's antenna quivered, because—whilst the words were casual—she knew that her husband was being careful with his response, and didn't want her delving any deeper. And so, she only nodded and remarked, "A stack of shell-companies, no doubt, so as to hide the true owner."

"It is the usual tactic."

Mental note, she thought; find out who's at the bottom of the limited companies. And—now that they were on the subject—she debated whether to inquire into the burnt-up coin shop, but decided she'd best retreat; her husband would want to know how she knew such a thing, and she didn't want to confess that Mary had passed along what Savoie had told her—that would only raise another dicey subject. And—speaking of dicey subjects—she needed to confess to Acton that she'd promised Mary she'd attend Howard's murder trial.

After hesitating for a moment, she decided to put-off this particular topic, also. He was not going to be happy about it—he was as private as they came, was Acton, and so was she, truth to tell. But in this instance he'd just have to get over it; it only made sense, that the fair Doyle should support her friend through the coming ordeal, and if it helped influence the jury to bring about justice for Howard, she shouldn't shrink from the spotlight. She'd wait for a better time to tell Acton, though—he still seemed balanced on a knife-edge, despite his best efforts to hide it from her.

With a pang of sympathy—it can't be easy, being someone like him and having to experience frustration in the same way that mere mortals did—she reached to lift his hand and kiss its back. "No tunnels, once we're home; you'll have to slip past the doorman to go walkin' a'nights."

He smiled, slightly. "I don't think it will be necessary. I am sorry, Kathleen, if I alarmed you."

"Whist," she replied. "I only wish I could help."

She waited a beat, but he was silent, and it was a bit concerning that he didn't think he could even respond to her gentle probing without her catching him out in some way. Therefore, with some firmness she advised, "Reynolds is goin' to stuff you full of food, husband. You're a bundle o' bones."

"If you insist," he replied, in a mild tone.

"Heavy, fattenin' things that are bad for you," she warned. "Bread-puddin', mayhap."

He tilted his head. "I cannot say that I care for bread-pudding."

She made a face. "No—no one does. Instead, we'll have ice cream—lots and lots."

"Done."

She smiled out the window, feeling somewhat better—especially since she was headed back to town where she'd still be on maternity leave but at least she could start working on this puzzle, as best as she was able.

Turning to her husband, she remarked, "It's so nice, to have a few minutes to ourselves whilst the boys are reticent."

"It is, indeed," he agreed.

CHAPTER 12

It was the next morning, and they were settling-in at home. Acton had gone to work early, and Doyle was seated at the kitchen table supervising Edward's breakfast, whilst Reynolds went through the cupboards, taking an inventory of what was needed for the get-back-up-to-speed shopping.

They lived in a spacious, two-story penthouse flat, located atop a posh residential building in Kensington. Such luxury was not really to Doyle's taste, but it was where Acton had lived as a bachelor and Acton was not one to want to move. The flat featured large picture windows that looked down upon the park across the street, and Doyle was contemplating the view with a great deal of fondness.

"It's good to be back," she observed to the servant. "Half the pleasure in goin' somewhere is the comin' home, again."

"Precisely, madam," Reynolds agreed.

"How was your holiday? Was it restful?"

"It was indeed, madam."

"Did you and Trenton go share a pint, and grouse about the boss?"

"I do not believe Mr. Trenton stayed in town, madam."

"Oh? Mayhap he went on another visit to Ireland; he and Lizzie went, once—which was rather surprisin', actually. I'll have to ask him." Lizzie Williams was Trenton's cousin, and they'd both originated from Acton's hereditary estate—which was the nearest thing to a cult, as far as Doyle could tell. It was positively medieval, the way the supporters of the House of Acton were loyal to a fault. For example, Lizzie worked in the forensics lab at the Met, and was often involved in Acton's shadowy doings since she was well-placed to do so.

"I believe Detective Munoz is visiting in Ireland, madam."

Doyle smiled to herself that Reynolds would keep tabs. He'd carried a mighty torch for Munoz before she got married—but, to be fair, so had everyone else with an XY chromosome. And it was somewhat ironic that the Spanish beauty had succumbed to a stolid Irish policeman in the end—it just went to show that love was mighty unpredictable. "Aye, that's right—it's the Irish relatives' turn to have a visit."

As she helped Edward put jam on another piece of toast—the boyo had a hollow leg, it seemed—Doyle informed Reynolds, "Mary and the girls came to visit for a few days. Acton thought it best to get her out of town for Howard's preliminary hearin'."

"A benevolent gesture; Lord Acton is very considerate, madam."

But Doyle was distracted, as she gazed out the window, because she was reminded of a troubling thought that had occurred to her at last night's feeding. Howard had asked Doyle to save Mary—she'd saved him once, he'd said, and now he wanted her to save Mary, too. The troubling thing, though, was that when the fair Doyle had saved Howard, she'd saved him from Acton.

At the time, Acton thought Howard was part of a government corruption rig—an earlier one than the Public Accounts scandal—but as it turned out, Howard was being framed-up since he was about to blow the whistle on the villains. Doyle had stepped in to stop Acton from arresting Howard, and the corruption rig had unwound from there, with a lot of high-ranking people being shuttled off to prison.

So—could it be, that Mary was in danger from *Acton*? Surely, that couldn't be it—why would Acton plan any harm to Mary? It would certainly explain why her husband was tied-up in knots, but why? Mary wasn't a criminal—Mary was a true believer, instead, and always saw the good in everybody, whether it was deserved or not. What had the ghost said? *Her ways are the ways of gentleness, and all her paths are peace.*

So, no; she was being fanciful—and a bit grim, all on account of her husband's being a bit grim. It was miles more likely that Howard was warning Doyle to save Mary from Savoie; it was that wolf-and-lamb thing, and she truly shouldn't put it off, any longer.

She winced, slightly, because she'd no idea how to bring up such a subject—not to mention, she wasn't sure how much she should tell Mary in the first place. Mary was already aware that Savoie had served a short stint at Wexton Prison—and so it wasn't as though she would be completely ignorant of the man's questionable past—but it seemed certain that she wouldn't know about the impressive length and breadth of his criminal doings. And it didn't help matters, of course, that Mary saw—and almost on a daily basis—that Savoie was friendly with the House of Acton and with Doyle in particular. So; in a way, it was doubly-important that the fair Doyle give her a bit of a warning.

It was something of a dilemma, though; Doyle didn't have a very good record as a matchmaker, and she didn't like the idea of attempting an un-match, either. Love was a powerful, powerful thing; awesome and unpredictable—as could be easily demonstrated by Doyle's own experience. She was therefore reluctant to put her foot in and attempt to second-guess it.

"Do you have a preference for the dinner menu tonight, madam?"

Brought back from her abstraction, Doyle advised, "Make sure to cook Acton somethin' hearty; the sea air wasn't good for the man's appetite."

"Is that so, madam? Perhaps a pasta dish, then."

"That sounds excellent."

Doyle checked the time. "Faith, Miss Valerie is goin' to be late for the first time in recorded history. It must be a sign o' the apocalypse."

"Perhaps there was a problem with the public transit this morning, madam."

"Mayhap." Leave it to the efficient nanny to be late on the one day that Doyle had plans.

"Lord Acton will not be home for lunch?"

"No—I'm takin' Tommy over to meet him for lunch. I'll be leavin' soon, as a matter of fact—I'm goin' over to show the baby to some of my friends at the Met."

"Very good, madam."

This proposed outing was actually an excuse to meet with Gabriel, for whatever-it-was he wanted to meet about, and to meet-up with Williams, too, so as to garner some needed information. Unfortunately, this promising plan would be stymied if Miss Valerie didn't show up soon. Everyone involved had competing schedules, including Tommy.

Whilst she tried to be patient, Doyle suddenly remembered another niggling loose-end. "Reynolds," she asked. "Who's Hector?"

The servant paused. "Hector, from the classics, madam?"

"I don't *know*," she replied, a bit crossly. "That's why I'm askin'."

"He was a famous warrior. From the Iliad."

"Oh. Is that the one about the Greeks?"

"Hector was a Trojan, madam. His rival, Achilles, was the Greek."

"Oh," she said, pondering this for a moment. "I suppose you'll have to remind me about the Iliad—what exactly happened?"

"It is rather a complicated story, madam." This, in the tone of one who is aware that his audience would not appreciate this fact.

She knit her brow. "Is it about vengeance?"

"Indeed, madam. In fact, Achilles killed Hector out of vengeance—although they both ended up dying in the end. Each character let his pride overcome everything he loved until there was nothing left."

Making a face of distaste, she observed, "That sounds a lot like that Shakespeare story—the one with that mopin' fellow, where everyone dies in the end."

"Exactly, madam; as a matter of fact, Shakespeare wrote another play, specifically about Achilles and Hector."

She raised her brows with interest. "Did he? Was it like the first one, with a ghost cryin' out for vengeance?"

"No—not the same at all, madam." The servant paused. "It was not as well-received, perhaps."

"Probably because it didn't have a ghost," she pointed out, in a practical manner. "People love a ghost-story. But tell me, Reynolds, was Hector the hero or the villain?"

"It is difficult to say, madam. Both Hector and Achilles were complex characters."

She frowned at him. "Well, there should be clear heroes and

clear villains, so that you know who you want to win. Someone needs to tell the Greeks how to write a decent story."

"Indeed, madam," the butler replied in a wooden tone.

Checking the time yet again, Doyle asked, "Could you phone Miss Valerie and check-in with her, Reynolds? I don't want to call, because I don't want her to think I'm annoyed. It seems so unlike her—she's usually so reliable; tends to show up early, as a matter of fact."

Reynolds dutifully rang-up the nanny, but reported, "Sent to voice-mail, madam."

Doyle blew out a breath. "Well, mayhap I *am* annoyed, after all."

"If you will allow me, madam, I will watch Edward, for you. I will save the shopping for when you return."

Brightening, Doyle lifted her face. "Oh—well, that's so kind of you Reynolds. And hopefully she'll show up soon, anyways."

"It will be my pleasure, madam—I have quite missed spending time alone with Edward."

This wasn't exactly true, but Doyle was not about to second-guess this unexpected boon, and so she hastily advised, "Let me fetch baby Tommy then, and we'll be off."

CHAPTER 13

*D*oyle was visiting Officer Gabriel in his office, tilting the chest-carrier so that the tall young man could get a glimpse of the sleeping baby as he stood behind her.

"He's got a nice head," Gabriel observed. "The top of it seems very sound. Is he an Earl, yet?"

"No—that's saved for Edward, and don't give Tommy any ideas or it will be like that famous story, with that dreadful woman."

"Which story is that? There are quite a few that feature dreadful women."

She smiled, "Faith, Gabriel; you sound like Acton. I mean the one where she prods her husband into murderin' the Earl—or whatever he was—so as to get the title." Brightening, she added, "There was a ghost in that one, too."

"*Macbeth*?" he ventured.

"Aye—that's it; a thoroughly dreadful woman, to steer her husband off the rails."

"She did go mad," he pointed out. "I confess there are times that I can relate to her, despite all her dreadfulness."

With some sympathy, Doyle asked, "How've you been, my friend?" He'd had a rough few years, had Gabriel, and his career had taken a slight detour due to a stint in rehab. But now he seemed hale, and she truly hoped his worst days were behind him.

"Overworked. Can you sit, with that thing?"

"I can." Doyle carefully lowered herself into the chair across from his desk, and duly noted that Gabriel casually walked over to close his office door before going around to seat himself. So; it seemed that whatever-it-was he wanted to say was a private matter.

As he settled-in behind his desk, he said, "First things first; you had a favor to ask?"

Reminded, Doyle stammered, "Oh—oh, yes; I wanted to review an autopsy report so as to see if a Code-Twenty had soot in the lungs, but now I don't need to." If a burnt body had no soot in the lungs, it meant the victim had been dead before the fire and the death was probably a homicide, as opposed to misadventure.

He raised his brows as he leaned back in this chair. "Well— don't leave me hanging; did they, or didn't they?"

"It turned out that it didn't really matter," she replied vaguely. Best watch her tongue; the last needful thing was to have Gabriel putting two and two together—he was a long-headed boyo, as past events had shown. She wasn't certain whether Acton wanted anyone to know about the actress-wrinkle, as yet—mainly because it seemed to her that her husband was wary, and stepping very carefully. Therefore, she rather hurriedly changed the subject. "Your turn."

He paused, and then said rather slowly, "I have been asked to give you a warning, and you must promise that you won't let on that it came from me."

She blinked in surprise, since—for once—he seemed rather somber. "Faith, that doesn't sound good."

He lifted a dark brow at her. "I don't know whether it is or it isn't, as yet. Hence, the warning."

"All right, then—hence, let's hear it."

"Nazy has a new boyfriend."

This was unexpected; Nazy was Acton's Assistant, a young Persian woman who was very organized when it came to calendaring and reports, even as she was a bit naïve when it came to people. "She does? Faith, I've been out of the loop."

"His name is Kian—a fellow Persian."

Doyle corrected, "You're only half."

"Point taken. Half a fellow-Persian, then."

With a small smile, she offered, "I suppose that's good news; Nazy had a massive crush on Sir Vikili, but he's gettin' married next week, so I'm happy she's come down to earth and found someone more suitable."

He cocked his head. "I think you're forgetting the part where this is a warning."

"Oh—oh; right. He's a bad 'un, this Kian?"

Gabriel nodded. "Apparently, Sir Vikili cannot be seen as involved, but he owes your husband a favor and so he has asked me to drop a word in your ear."

This did seem a bit ominous—that Sir Vikili had felt it necessary—and so Doyle sombered in turn. "What do we know?"

But her companion only spread his hands. "I am not aware; I'm just the messenger. But, if I ignore Sir Vikili I'll be cast out of the community."

Doubtfully, she knit her brow. "I never had the impression that you're much-involved in that community."

He amended, "If I ignore Sir Vikili, I will never win another case."

"That's miles more believable," she agreed. "So; you don't know why the warnin'?"

"I do not."

This was not exactly true, and she decided to let him see, by her silence, that she was skeptical.

However, he insisted, "No—really. And it's not just that the fellow cut me out with Nazy."

She made a wry mouth. "The likes of you aren't goin' to fall in love with Nazy, Gabriel."

"Is that so? Well, I should—just to show that you don't know me half as well as you think you do."

She observed, "I think no one knows you very well."

With a smile, he shrugged. "A fair point, I suppose."

"Thank you, for the warnin'," she said, as she carefully rose to her feet again. "I will set the wheels in motion." It was clear that the intended recipient for this message was Acton, but this rather obvious fact would not be spoken aloud.

"You didn't hear it from me," her reminded her, as he rose to cross over to the door.

"I'll think of a plausible tale; I'm meetin' my husband, for lunch."

He made a sound of regret, as he opened the door. "I wish I was somebody's husband."

"It does seem as though Nazy's goin' to be available again," she teased, as she walked through the door.

Doyle then made her way to Williams' office, which was on the same floor, but she had to pause a few times to show the baby to the admiring staff, who knew on which side their bread was buttered, and therefore had wonderful praise for the Chief Inspector's new baby.

As she smiled, and responded, Doyle couldn't help but feel a wash of sympathy for Gabriel. He was another one who'd been madly in love with Detective Munoz, but Munoz had rather unexpectedly married Inspector Geary, and Gabriel—despite his light words—was still a bit thrown off his pins about it.

As she paused outside of Williams' door, Doyle tried to decide how she would feel if Acton had broken it off with her and then married someone else at the CID. It would be the next thing to unbearable, she decided; and she'd promptly find another job— probably far away. Interesting, that Gabriel still hung 'round such a painful environment—one would think he could retreat back to MI 5 any time he wished.

With a sigh, she put Gabriel's problems from her mind and girded her loins for the next item on her list of things to do.

CHAPTER 14

*I*nspector Thomas Williams was Doyle's closest friend; their relationship was complicated, a bit, by the fact that he was one of Acton's most loyal henchman here at the Met, and therefore never hesitated to help her husband mete-out a rough justice for any villain who'd managed to escape a reckoning.

Since Doyle took a dim view of vigilantism, they tended to avoid certain topics so that they wouldn't come to cuffs—although they still did, on occasion. Despite this, Williams was a loyal friend, and had her back—as he'd proved on many an occasion.

"Sorry I'm a bit late," Doyle apologized, as she settled into his office chair. "We had nanny problems."

"Your nannies always bring the drama," he reminded her, as he closed-out his laptop.

"Not this one; she's drama-free. But I left Reynolds in charge of Edward, so hopefully she's managed to show up."

Doyle paused, because it seemed likely that she'd have heard this, if it had happened, and so she could probably presume it had not. "I should check-in with the poor man, but I have to go down the list with you, first, because I'm in need of information and this is my one chance."

With a smile, he leaned back in his chair. "Fire away, Kath."

Since she was on a baby-feeding deadline, Doyle cut down to brass tacks. "Have you heard any rumors about any major players from the Public Accounts scandal who've managed to slip the net?"

He raised his brows. "No."

This was the truth, and it was interesting; it meant that Williams was not aware of whatever-it-was that was keeping Acton up at nights.

Intrigued, he straightened-up and crossed his arms on the desk. "What have you heard?"

She drew a breath, trying to decide how much to say—she was a gabbler by nature, and so parsing words was never her strong suit. "I think Acton is unhappy about the way it's landed, but he's bein' mighty tight-lipped about it. Which makes me think that someone's still out there."

"Charbonneau?" he suggested. "Although she was more a foot-soldier than a major player."

"Acton seems to think Charbonneau is dead."

Williams gazed out the window as he considered this. "Possibly. It would explain why we haven't caught a glimpse of her, despite the APW."

"Hers may have been a containment-murder, which is one of the things that makes me think there must be another player out there, busily coverin'-up. That, and the burnt yachts."

He returned his interested gaze to her. "Fill me in, on the burnt yachts."

Surprised, she said, "Oh—there was a fire at Heaton Marina, in

Bristol, when we were stayin' near there. Some of the yachts they used for smugglin' were torched, and there was a Code-Twenty." She paused. "You haven't heard?"

"No—and I'm not sure why I would. That's not our jurisdiction, Kath."

Slowly, she offered, "But Acton—and the local precinct—seem to think it's somehow connected to the Public Accounts case; hence my interest in any major players who haven't yet been rolled-up." Privately, she was rather pleased that Gabriel had reminded her about the word "hence," since it was one of those words that made a person sound very smart.

"Really? I haven't been briefed," he admitted.

"Well, keep it under your hat, but I imagine you will be; Acton wants to verify the ID of the Code-Twenty first, before he moves on it."

"Who does he think it is?"

"That actress who's gone missing—Sasha Lanska."

But Williams' reaction was completely unexpected, as he stared at her in acute dismay. "Holy *Christ*."

Surprised in turn, she scolded, "You mustn't blaspheme, Thomas. What? D'you know somethin'?"

"I know her," he admitted.

Oh-oh, thought Doyle, with a sinking heart. "And how is that, my friend?"

He was profoundly distracted, and contemplated his desk top for a moment. "She came forward with some information on one of my cases."

With a great deal of misgiving, Doyle prompted, "And?"

He'd recovered from his surprise, and shrugged slightly as he met her eyes. "It wasn't a big deal; I had a couple of drinks with her, once."

She drew down her brows.

"All right," he admitted, "twice." Williams was the only other person, save Acton, who knew about Doyle's truth-detecting abilities.

Very much dismayed, Doyle pointed out, "Lizzie's not someone who would handle that very well, Thomas." Williams had married Lizzie, the young woman who worked for Acton in the forensics lab.

He closed his eyes briefly, at this reference to his wife. "I know —I know. And I cut it off, anyway—I had to start ignoring Sasha's texts. She seemed a little too interested, for someone like her."

Fairly, Doyle observed, "Well she's older, and you're a handsome boyo, Thomas. Was she married at the time?"

"No—no, of course not."

He seemed stung by the question, and in all exasperation Doyle pointed out, "Well—lest we forget—you were."

He turned up his hands. "I didn't seek her out, Kath; she came forward on a case. She's famous, and—and it was flattering, I guess. But like I said, she was a little too persistent, and it set off alarm bells."

"When was this? Hopefully, you won't be showin' up on a list of her known-associates."

"I doubt it—it was months ago."

"Well, she was bad news, my friend. Acton says she was a member of some mafia group, the Mosso-somethin'."

"The Mossovet. It's not the mafia, it's a political group, and she'd already dropped out before she contacted me. Don't worry, I did a search on her."

There was a small silence, and then Doyle ventured, "D'you think a touch of marriage-counselin' might be in order?"

But he only gave her a look. "Don't go there, Kath."

"Right," she hastily agreed. "None o' my business." Williams had rather unexpectedly found himself married to his wife, and—

despite the unexpectedness—it seemed to be working out. Although if he was stepping-out with actresses, Doyle may have to reevaluate this assessment.

"And speakin' of such, how's our Lizzie feelin'?" she asked, a bit pointedly. Lizzie was in the middle stages of pregnancy.

"She's feeling better now, but things were rough for a while, between Connor, and Mary Howard needing her help, and the dry-labbing investigation."

Doyle blinked. "No clue, what that last one's about."

He nodded. "I'm not surprised—it's been kept fairly quiet. Forensics was falsifying records and not doing the actual lab-work on a number of cases. It's still unclear whether it was out of laziness, or to tamper with evidence. If it was deliberate, of course, we'd have a major scandal on our hands—which is why it's been kept quiet."

Very much dismayed, Doyle observed, "Recall that the tip-line people were part-and-parcel of the Public Accounts corruption rig. Faith, it looks as though the villains were coverin' themselves by usin' people from both ends of any investigation, so as to quash any and all problems."

He nodded in agreement. "Right; it doesn't look good for the personnel involved. That, and the fact that the fentanyl evidence has gone missing."

Doyle blinked, yet again. "The *fentanyl* evidence from Nigel Howard's case? Holy Mother, Thomas; how could that go missin'?"

"It's unclear, since the evidence logs show it was inventoried in the Evidence Locker." He gave her a look.

"Fancy that," she replied with some irony. Unfortunately, whenever narcotics were stored as evidence,they were prone to go missing; a great deal of money could be made, and the temptation for the office personnel was often too much. "Faith, Howard's trial's just around the corner; what will they do?"

He shrugged. "The prosecution will have to rely on the autopsy results, along with circumstantial evidence."

She knit her brow, thinking this over. "It should still be an airtight case."

"You'd think so. But it doesn't look good, that the main evidence has gone missing."

"I remember that Lizzie was askin' Mary if she'd given all the pills to the police," Doyle mused. "So; that was why."

"Yes. That's what the dry-labbing investigation is all about; if the lab personnel are compromised, it may turn out that a lot of cases are tainted. The higher-ups have to be careful about how they handle this."

"Because the public shouldn't lose trust in the institutions," she filled in with a touch of scorn. "Which is a pack of nonsense—best to make a clean breast, and let the chips fall where they may."

"Acton takes a different view," he reminded her.

With a mighty effort, she reined-in her temper. "I know, and before I hale off on a lecture I'll pull my horns in, and instead ask you for a couple of favors before Tommy, here, starts howlin'."

But DI Williams had learned a few lessons from his granting-favors experiences, and he cocked his head. "Let's hear them, first."

"Well, first off, I'm lookin' to find out who held ownership of the yachts that were burnt."

He was immediately wary. "And why can't you ask Acton?"

"I did, and he gave me one of his patented non-answers."

"Then I'll have to pass, Kath," he replied, rather firmly.

"You've divided loyalties," she conceded. "Fair enough. Well, here's somethin' you won't object to, I hope. I'd like to do a follow-up visit with both the bakery and the transport company from the Public Accounts case. I know they've arrested the conspirators who were working there, but I'd like to poke about a bit more, to gauge whether there could be someone else who has indeed slipped the net."

But he only raised his brows. "You haven't heard? The bakery had a fire, and had to close down."

She stared at him in astonishment, unable to find her voice for a moment. "Well, that can't be a coincidence, my friend."

"Really? You think it's connected to the yachts?"

"The coin shop in Bristol burnt down, too."

Thoughtfully, he met her eyes. "Has it? Then it does sound as though your theory may be correct—someone has slipped the net, and is covering their tracks."

"Will you take me over to the transport company, then?"

Making a decision, he replied, "All right. But I can't allot more than an hour or two—the investigation is closed, and I don't want to re-open the budget."

"Thanks, Thomas—I don't think it will take very long; I just feel as though I should do a bit of follow-up."

"Always a pleasure, Kath," he replied.

CHAPTER 15

Having completed her tasks for the morning, Doyle gently jostled baby Tommy—who was starting to get hungry—and made her way over to Acton's office to meet-up for their planned lunch.

He pinged her just as she was getting off the lift, and she so she raised her phone, jostling the baby carrier with a bit more gusto as she did so. "Ho, husband—I'm a bit late, but I'm comin'."

"Please don't rush on my account. Do you mind if I meet with the Assistant DCI, for a few minutes? It is something that should be done in person."

That dry-labbing scandal, Doyle surmised. Poor Acton, to have to try to stamp out that prairie-fire just as he's back from holiday. "No worries, Tommy needs feedin' and hence, I'll nip into your office to keep him reticent." *Good* one, Doyle.

"Thank you."

He rang off, and Doyle sheathed her mobile, thinking that this was actually a happy turn of events since she would be given a prime opportunity to ask a few questions of Nazy-of-the-smoky-beau.

"Ho, Nazy," Doyle greeted the girl as she approached her desk, which was situated in the hallway outside Acton's office. "Acton's runnin' late, so I'm goin' to feed the baby in his office."

Nazy smiled cheerfully. "Very good, Officer Doyle."

Doyle teased, "I'm that surprised you're not dressed in mournin', what with Sir Vikili gettin' himself married."

The girl laughed. "I am happy that he is happy, Officer Doyle."

"Now, that's a good attitude to have."

"It helps that I have a boyfriend," the girl disclosed, her eyes shining.

"Do you? Tell me all about this lucky fellow, then—come in with me, I've got to get to Tommy before he melts down."

Doyle hoisted the baby out of his carrier as she settled down in one of Acton's visitor's chairs, whilst Nazy—rather hesitantly—edged over to sit in the other.

Oh, thought Doyle a bit belatedly; I probably shouldn't be flashing my bosom at Nazy-of-the-hijab. Therefore, with more discretion than was her usual, Doyle turned aside slightly as she lifted her shirt, and put the baby to breast.

"He is a beautiful baby," Nazy offered, in the tone of someone who believes her own babies are just around the corner.

Yikes, thought Doyle; poor Nazy. Aloud, she teased, "So, tell me all about this new boyo. Is he as handsome as Sir Vikili?"

"No one is," laughed Nazy. "But he is good-looking." She added a bit shyly, "He is very nice to me."

"That's what's important," Doyle agreed. "How did the two of you meet?"

Nazy smiled happily. "It was a chance meeting, Officer Doyle. The Chief Inspector wished me to deliver an envelope to Mrs. Williams, on a morning when she helping-out at Mrs. Howard's flat. Kian works at the security desk in Mrs. Howard's building, and so we began talking."

"It was fate," Doyle decreed.

"Indeed, it was," Nazy agreed happily.

Casually, Doyle kept her gaze on baby Tommy and asked, "Is Kian interested in your work here, Nazy?

"Oh, yes; he was very saddened to hear of Mr. Howard's death. He is happy that the trial will be finally underway."

Well, thought Doyle fairly; that's not too surprising—if the fellow knew Howard, and saw him coming in and out every day. But Sir Vikili wouldn't be going to all the trouble of making a roundabout warning unless there was a problem, here.

Aloud, she offered, "You can't speak of Acton's cases to him, you know."

"Oh—no, Officer Doyle; I know better than that," Nazy agreed. Her phone then pinged, and she checked it. "Mrs. Williams is here to deliver a file. If you will excuse me?"

"Send her in," said Doyle. "I've somethin' to say to her."

And so, a few minutes later, Nazy ushered-in Lizzie Williams who smiled as she beheld Doyle, feeding baby Tommy. "Hallo, Lady Acton."

"Hallo, Lizzie. I'm sorry to nab you, but I wanted to speak to you if you have a moment."

"Certainly," the other young woman agreed, and then sat down on the chair Nazy had just vacated.

Doyle duly noted that she'd just heard of two instances where Lizzie was delivering paper documents to Acton in person, rather than sending them electronically. So; a person could conclude that, whatever the illustrious Chief Inspector was having Lizzie do for him, it was being kept mighty private.

Doyle began, "I'm hearin' from Nazy that she's datin' a young man who works in Mary's buildin'."

Lizzie knit her brow. "Is she? I didn't know."

Doyle explained, "I was going to ask what you knew about him—she's a bit naïve." Doyle paused. "He's a Persian fellow, and he works at the security desk."

"Oh—oh, yes." Lizzie paused, as though debating what to say. "He was rather flirtatious, actually."

"With *you*?" This was a surprise—Lizzie wasn't unattractive, but she was rather no-nonsense—and Doyle rather belatedly realized she shouldn't have expressed her incredulity quite so openly.

But Lizzie only offered a faint smile. "With me."

Cautiously, Doyle ventured, "Was this before or after he met our Nazy?"

"I can't say. I told him I was married, and made it clear I wasn't interested."

This was just the opening that Doyle was looking for, and so she seized it with both hands. "Yes, well—that brings me to my next topic. I know you've been run ragged betwixt your adopted son, and the new baby on the way—not to mention having to organize the evidence for the murder trial—but don't forget to make time for your husband, Lizzie."

Understandably, her companion stared at her in abject surprise, but Doyle plunged on; the young woman had once asked Doyle for sex-advice—such as it was—and it seemed that she was in sore need of yet another dose. "Acton's on his way, and I've haven't the time to beat about the bush. Pull out your spiky-heeled boots and take the man to bed—this isn't complicated, Lizzie."

The other girl's eyes narrowed. "What have you heard?"

"He's not havin' an affair, or anythin'; I just caught the sense that he feels a bit neglected. Put Connor to bed, and bake him somethin'—preferably naked. He loves your cookin', and for men, that counts for a lot." She paused, thinking this over. "You may want to pretend you've burnt your fingers, so as to get within strikin' distance."

There was a small pause, and then Lizzie offered in a dry tone, "I appreciate the advice, Lady Acton, but it is not as though ours is a love match."

"Then make it so," Doyle advised, with some exasperation.

CHAPTER 16

*L*izzy left, and Doyle shifted Tommy to the other side as she juggled her mobile on her knee, ringing up Acton on his work-line—as opposed to their personal line, so that he'd know it wasn't anything important if he was still in his meeting. She half-expected to be sent to voicemail, but he answered. "Kathleen."

"Any chance we can skip lunch, and nip over to our favorite hotel?"

"There is every chance," he replied immediately.

"Best order room service, though—I'm starvin'."

"I will pick you up in front."

"Give me twenty minutes, I'm finishin'-up with Tommy."

"Done."

She smiled, as she zipped the now-sleepy Tommy back into his carrier. She'd no spiky-heeled black boots at hand, but Acton wasn't one who needed much prompting in the first place.

Walking out into the hallway she asked, "Nazy, would you mind checkin' on somethin' for me? I've been far too busy."

"Of course, Officer Doyle."

"I'd like to look up who owns a yacht. It's called the *Sophia*, and it was destroyed in a fire, recently. The report should be filed with the local precinct, in Bristol."

Nazy, who was a wizard at such things, pulled up the record in a matter of moments, and Doyle leaned over her shoulder so as to read the screen.

"The owner is a limited company, Officer Doyle."

"Can we see who the principals are?"

As Nazy delved into the publicly-listed personnel, she noted, "Oh—the company's representative for service-of-process is Sir Vikili."

"Is it? Well, good for him, to be hangin' about with the fancy-yachts crowd."

Nazy clicked a bit further, and announced, "The principal officer is a man named Igor Denisovich."

Ah—the dead woman's ex-husband, Doyle thought. Curiouser and curiouser—why would Acton not want me to know this? It seems that our Mr. Denisovich owned this yacht and held a grudge against his ex-wife—which would be pertinent, one would think, if one were a detective, and considering things like motive and opportunity.

But it also meant that the fair Doyle could be jumping at shadows; it was entirely plausible that Sir Vikili had come to the morgue so as to monitor whether his client's name would come up, with respect to the arson-fire-with-a-dead-body-thrown-in. Which would be a perfectly reasonable thing for a solicitor to do.

But with a mental sigh, Doyle admitted that—whilst at first glance, it might seem so—such was obviously not the case. There was something here that her husband very much didn't want her to find out. But—sad to say—the poor man's wants were doomed to failure, due to a friendly ghost who was wanting the exact opposite.

"Thanks, Nazy," Doyle said brightly. "That's very helpful." One of the good things about Nazy was that it wouldn't occur to her to wonder why Acton's wife was researching a case whilst she was on maternity leave. It was all rather ironic, actually; Doyle didn't dare do the research at home for fear that Acton would find it, but he'd never think that she'd do it right under his nose—so to speak—by using Nazy. Another good one, Doyle.

Once they'd arrived at the hotel suite, Doyle and Acton decided that Tommy's hotel-crib could be pushed into the bathroom suite—as long as the door was left ajar—and then they fell into the bed with no further ado. They came to the trusty Grenoble Hotel, from time to time, so as to have a respite from the various butlers-and-nannies who were necessarily underfoot at home. And the discreet staff, here at the posh hotel, never indicated in any fashion that they were aware of the reason Lord and Lady Acton would want to be alone for an hour or two, during the midday.

After a leisurely session of love-making, Doyle lay beside her husband in the nest of rumpled bedclothes and whispered, "Good one, to remember that we would need a crib."

"We could always put him in the bathtub, I suppose. He's not going anywhere."

She propped herself up to kiss his chest, her hair falling in a curtain around her face. "Good one on Tommy, to sleep in a strange place."

"A commendable baby."

"A commendable husband," she teased, and nibbled at him. "D'you want to talk business, or save it for later? I don't want to spoil the mood."

"I will talk about whatever you wish. I need time to regroup."

She laughed. "Hence."

"Hence," he agreed, and pulled her head to his so as to kiss her. "What's on your mind?"

"I've been asked to give you a warnin', but not to tell you who told me."

He raised his brows. "Let's hear it."

"Nazy's new beau is trouble, apparently. Sir Vikili wanted to drop a word in your ear, but he couldn't do it directly and so instead he used a cut-out." The relationship betwixt Acton and Sir Vikili was as complex as it was fascinating; they were allies and they were enemies, and they could almost never speak directly with each other about anything that was important.

He raised his brows. "Kian? I did do a background check."

"Of course, you did; but apparently there's somethin' you missed." She paused, debating whether to relate what Lizzie had said, and then compromised, "I asked Lizzie about this Kian fellow—since he works at Mary's buildin'—and she didn't seem to have a good impression."

"I will look into it," he agreed.

Doyle sighed, as she turned her head to gaze out the window for a moment. "Poor Nazy. She's a bit like Gabriel—unlucky in love. I was thinkin' about what I'd do, if you dropped me like a hot brick and then married someone else in the department."

He smiled, as he drew out a tendril of her hair, letting it fall to her shoulder. "And what would you do?"

"Find a new job, and move somewhere far away. I wonder if the Yorkshire Dales has need of a new detective?"

He gathered her up into his arms, and she settled-in beside him. "Fortunately, not at all necessary."

"Very fortunately."

She lay against his shoulder, content to continue gazing out the window at the fading afternoon sunlight. "You know, Michael, when Sir Vikili showed up at the morgue, d'you think he was tryin' to warn you about somethin', even though he couldn't speak of what-ever-it-was?"

"Warn me of what?"

"I don't know, but mayhap it was like this warnin' that he gave about Nazy's beau; he can't say anythin' directly, but he showed up at the morgue because he wanted you to stay sharp, and pay attention."

He thought about this, for a moment. "It is possible."

"Recall that we think a major player is still on the loose," she ventured.

"Yes. But I will ask you to allow me to handle it, Kathleen."

She tilted her head to look at him. "You're bein' mighty mysterious, husband. And it's wearin' you to a thread, I might add."

His chest rose and fell. "The dental records positively identified Sasha Lanska. No soot in the lungs."

"So; we've got ourselves a homicide."

He nodded. "I would like to interview the ex-husband—perhaps as early as tomorrow morning, if that is agreeable."

"Happy to be of service," Doyle replied, even as she noted that he'd deftly changed the subject when she started probing about the player who was still at-large. She was getting better at noticing; in the old days, he'd have sent her off on the wrong track as easy as a tinker's pitch, but nowadays, she was wise to his wily ways.

He closed his eyes—he was a bit sleepy, which was a good thing. He was still too thin and not sleeping well, and she knew that this state of affairs was directly connected to his deft change-of-subject; someone out there had slipped the net, and it was giving him fits.

She thought about it as she idly pulled at the hair on his chest.

The main reason she'd put two-and-two together was because Howard's ghost had shown up, politely asking for vengeance. It just stood to reason—he'd not be doing such a thing, if all of his killers were safely rolled-up and awaiting trial.

And it also seemed clear that Acton was stymied about it, for some reason. No, not exactly stymied—she'd plenty of experience with stymied-Acton, but this was different; he wasn't so much stymied, as he was brooding—and—and *angry*. It was a dangerous combination, and she was suddenly reminded about what he'd said about King David's scorched-earth response at Ziklag. Was Acton bent on vengeance, too? Why? And for what?

Frowning, she stilled her hand and considered this. The ghost had also said that she should go back to the very beginning—but the beginning of what? When she'd first met Howard? She'd met Howard during a visit to Trestles; he was in some sort of administrative position with the government, and he was honing-in on the old government corruption rig. The villains had turned 'round and framed him up so as to cook his goose, but Acton had turned the tables—in true Acton-fashion—and got the villains cooked, instead.

And then Howard had run for MP, and got engaged to Lady Abby—now, there was a crazy-bird, and a perfect example of how men lost their bearings when it came to a pretty face. But—in the nick of time—Howard met sweet Mary, broke it off with Abby, and married Mary. So; what "beginning" was the ghost referring to? It was all water under the bridge, certainly—the government corruption players from that first scandal were all in prison, and Lady Abby was dead. Was he saying that there were still some people out there—people who held a mighty grudge and were plotting to murder him, all this time later? It was possible.

With a knit brow, she asked aloud, "Was there anyone from

Howard's old corruption scandal who's got out of prison, recently?"

If her husband was surprised by the introduction of this random topic, he hid it well. "The DCS?"

She made a wry mouth. "Well, that's not it."

"Not what?"

"I'm just playin' with the possibility—hear me out, husband—that these Public Accounts defendants weren't clever enough to pull-off the tainted-medication murders; it never made much sense, to me. Mayhap the "someone" who's still out there is the one who actually killed Howard."

"An independent actor? That seems unlikely, Kathleen."

Oh-ho, she thought with some surprise; hit the nail on the head, I have.

CHAPTER 17

"*I*t was just a thought," Doyle continued in a casual tone. "I just wondered if it was a possibility, that someone from the old case—someone who's nursin' a mighty grudge—may have actually been behind it, instead of the defendants who are goin' to trial."

"They've already held the Plea and Trial Preparation Hearing," he reminded her. "The court found there was enough evidence to bind these defendants over for trial."

Since this brought up another dicey subject in what seemed to be an unending list of them, Doyle mentally girded her loins. "Yes, well—speakin' of the trial, Mary asked if I would mind sittin' with her."

There was a pause. "I do not think it a good idea, Kathleen."

"I knew you wouldn't," she confessed. "But I didn't know what else to say."

"Allow me to have a word with the Crown Prosecutor, then."

"I'm the famous bridge-jumper," she lamented. "'Tis a heavy burden to bear."

"I will suggest a statement for the media, instead," he offered. "As you are a new mother."

"Don't be annoyed with Mary, please; I'm sure it was the prosecution, leanin' on her."

"No doubt."

He was not happy about this turn of events, as she'd known he wouldn't be. The last thing Acton would want was to have his wife featured, front-and-center, in a sensational murder trial. Emotions were running high since the crime was a despicable one, with nine innocent people losing their lives in the scheme. It was similar to the outcry that arose when they were dealing with a serial killer; it brought home the sad fact—so often suppressed, by the general population—that life was a dangerous proposition, no matter the precautions one took.

He was quiet, for a space of time, and it seemed he'd fallen asleep—his breathing deepened as they lay here together, in the warmth of the comfortable bed. Good, a snatch of sleep was just what the man needed; it must be exhausting work, trying to keep whatever-it-was away from his probing wife, who had such an unfair advantage.

In a sudden moment of clarity, she realized what she should have realized straightaway if she hadn't been burdened with new-baby brain. After all, she'd seen this particular morality-play often enough, and she was a crackin' knocker not to recognize the same old script: they were dealing with a despicable crime, Acton had conceded that not all the players had been rolled-up, she'd the strong feeling that he knew exactly who the remaining player was —the one who'd killed Howard—but in the meantime, he was fending-off her questions.

Faith, the answer was staring her in the face; in true Acton-fashion, her husband was planning to serve-up some home-brewed justice on the unsuspecting player—who was probably congratulating himself that he'd managed to get away. It was obvious—or it should have been obvious, if she'd been paying half-attention.

And small wonder, that he wanted her to remain ignorant of his plans. She could argue till she was blue in the face about the evils of vigilante justice, and how they were sworn to uphold the law, but—despite the things he'd say so as to soothe her—she knew that it never made much of a dent; he felt very comfortable in his role as a righter-of-wrongs. She may be his emergency brake —the only person on earth who could convince him to temper his actions—but without that brake he'd speed straight ahead, untroubled.

Although, this time, it seemed different—he was indeed troubled, this time around. His vigilante-planning wasn't making him keenly satisfied, which was his usual mode-of-operation. Usually, he was—he was very much *alive*, for want of a better word; like one of his ancestors would be in preparing for battle. But this time, he didn't seem quite so keen.

She could hear Tommy begin to make the little noises that babies make when they are wondering where the foodwagon is, and so she carefully slid out of bed, and tiptoed into the bathroom, quietly closing the door behind her. Acton wouldn't sleep long—he wasn't much of a napper, by nature—but she'd let him go for as long as she could.

Fifteen minutes later, she was holding Tommy in the dark, seated on the edge of the tub when Acton opened the bathroom door. "Come out where it is more comfortable, please."

"We are perfectly comfortable, my friend." She pronounced it "paarfectly" so as to tease him. "Go back to sleep."

He ran his hands over his face. "As delightful as that sounds, I've several meetings, lined up."

"Of course you do, poor you. And you never ate anythin', either. Shame on me, for feedin' your lust, instead."

He smiled, and leaned to kiss her. "I'll ask for a carton of fruit and cheese, to pick up at the parking garage. What would you like?"

"Nothin'—I'll fend for myself, at home. Coffee," she amended. "The coffee here is crackin' good."

"I'll shower; when you are ready, I will drop you home."

She warned, "Don't think you're weaselin' out on another go, tonight, husband. I've been short-changed and I demand my due."

He leaned to kiss her again, in a lingering fashion. "Willingly."

Good one, Doyle, she thought; a bit more canoodling tonight will soften him up, so that I can try to winkle-out from him exactly who he's goin' after, and why. Mother a' Mercy, but it's guileful work being the emergency brake.

CHAPTER 18

 hen Doyle arrived home with Tommy, it was to discover that Miss Valerie had never shown up.

"I am afraid that I could not raise her, madam," Reynolds explained with a tinge of disapproval. Reynolds was not one to tolerate haphazard work amongst his fellow servants.

But Doyle was having a hard time believing that Miss Valerie could be haphazard in the first place. "D'you think she got her dates mixed up? Or didn't realize that we'd be back home, already?"

"If that were the case, madam, it seems unusual that she'd not take my call."

This was a good point, and she eyed him. "Should we call the agency?"

"I thought I'd defer to you, madam."

Doyle could see his dilemma. If there was a harmless explanation, they didn't want to get the woman in trouble with the top-notch agency—and besides, it would feel as though they were snitching behind her back, which was not a good start for the sort of relationship one needed with one's nanny.

"D'you think she just up and quit, without even a by-your-leave? Faith, Williams was just sayin' that our nannies always bring the drama, and here we are yet again. Let's give it a day, and try to raise her again tomorrow; if we can't, then I think we've no choice but to call the agency. In the meantime, d'you think we could schedule Callie to handle Tommy tomorrow mornin'? I don't want to impose on the lass, but I know Acton wants me to go on a witness interview, and I *truly* shouldn't bring the baby."

"I will ask Miss Callie, madam. And before I forget, Miss Nellie called from the church. She said it was not urgent, but when you had a moment."

"Oh—wonder what that's about?" Nellie was Father John's church administrator, and an old friend of Doyle's. "Thanks, Reynolds, you've been holdin' the fort on all fronts. How was our Edward?"

"I arranged to take him to the park, madam, to play with Miss Gemma for an hour."

Doyle smiled, because Edward was deep into his afternoon nap. "A good strategy, my friend. Was Emile there, too?"

"No, madam; neither Master Emile nor Mr. Savoie was in attendance. I did meet Mrs. Mackey, however."

Doyle raised her brows. "Oh—oh, that's right; she said she was comin' into town, on holiday. A nice woman."

"Very pleasant. She had kind words for you and Lord Acton, certainly."

Reminded, Doyle asked in a casual tone, "Did you meet Jamie?"

"And who is Jamie, madam?"

Vaguely, Doyle offered, "One of her children, I think—she was going to stay with them, whilst she was in town."

He frowned, slightly. "I did not gain the impression that Mrs. Mackey has children, madam."

"Oh—oh, I must be mixed-up, then."

So; the mystery deepened with respect to the housekeeper at The Mermaid Inn. A bit crossly, Doyle thought—I honestly can't allow myself to be any more distracted than I already am; I've research to do, and I've got to quit jumping down rabbit-holes every time I turn around.

And so, with no further ado, Doyle sat down and began to research Sasha Lanska, having the rare opportunity to do so whilst both boys were asleep. There was quite a bit, of course; the woman had been a celebrated actress for nearly twenty years. She was attractive without being beautiful—which seemed to be a prerequisite, for famous stage actresses—and she'd performed in quite a few plays—most of which Doyle had never heard of, but which were apparently well-received by the theatre crowd.

Her personal life was a bit more straightforward than the usual famous-actress bio; she'd been born near St. Petersburg—there it was, again; that St Petersburg connection—and she'd immigrated to England when she'd first started her career.

Interestingly enough, she'd been arrested, a time or two— malicious mischief, with no specifics given. This was a "general" crime that covered a wide variety of bad acts, from graffiti to vandalism, and other miscellaneous damage to property. So; she'd been a bit wild, when she was younger. She'd married only once, to Igor Denisovich, and they'd divorced a few years ago—rather acrimoniously, with accusations of infidelity thrown back and forth. Since then, she'd dated a variety of men—some low-profile and some high-profile—but she didn't seem to have a steady boyfriend, which was a shame; steady boyfriends tended to be obvious suspects when you were dealing with a victim who might be termed promiscuous.

Thinking about this, she hoped they would not be called-upon to interview Williams as a "last-seen"; now, wouldn't that be a sticky wicket?

Doyle then logged onto the confidential police database—which would have even more information that was not accessible to the public—and saw that what Acton had intimated was true; Sasha had been a bit radical, in her politics—although to be fair, this was rather in keeping with the theatre crowd. She'd belonged to that Mossovet organization, which was apparently one that the Home Office tended to keep an eye on.

Doyle paused, because this suddenly struck her as a bit strange; the Russian mafia-types tended to pose as businessmen, rather than radical-politics people. Because there was a very fine line between sharp business practices and outright crime, they were usually very slippery, and granted the police no favors by openly skirting the law or otherwise drawing attention to themselves. The men who wound-up atop the underworld heap tended to be very good at avoiding any legal repercussions, and it was no coincidence that a top-notch solicitor like Sir Vikili featured prominently in this Denisovich fellow's doings.

So; it didn't make a lot of sense. If Denisovich was Russian mafia, he'd be very unhappy—one would think—to have his high-profile wife so active in a political group that tended to draw Home Office attention. Even more strange was the fact that Sasha had left the group about the same time she divorced her husband. You'd think she would go the opposite way, and throw herself even more whole-heartedly into it without the disapproving husband at her elbow.

Doyle then turned to Denisovich, who could have been the poster-child for a Russian mafia-type. He was a sleek man in his fifties, currently single, who owned a series of limited companies similar to the one that owned the burnt yachts, with always the same rotating handful of people in control. But creating shell-companies was no crime, of course, and in fact, a lot of Russian businessmen had been doing just that to buy-up posh properties in London, lately. Indeed, Acton had mentioned that such a group had tried to buy their own building about a year or so ago, but the owners had politely declined—no doubt aided by the fact that this was about the same time Acton was shoveling cash at them so as to purchase their own second floor.

She looked into Denisovich's list of known-associates, and duly noted that one of them was Philippe Savoie—another name that made the Watch List types nervous. This did not necessarily mean anything, in and of itself; it could be presumed that all the criminal kingpins knew one another—and sometimes came to cuffs—but still, it was of interest.

Of course, there was a simple explanation for it; when Savoie had first come to London it was to take-over Solonik's smuggling rig, and Solonik had been connected to Denisovich all the way back to St. Petersburg. As was often the case with such things, there would be no grudges held when a lucrative rig was at stake, and it wouldn't be a stretch to assume that Savoie and Denisovich had become business partners, with Savoie slipping into Solonik's role after the Russian man had been killed.

This thought only served to remind Doyle that she *truly* must speak to Mary about Savoie, no matter how awkward the conversation. Howard had tasked the fair Doyle with saving Mary, and the only possible threat to Mary that Doyle could see, was the relationship the young woman was rapidly developing with Savoie. Although—to be fair—it might just be that the ghost was unhappy that any man was looking to take his place, and so soon.

Doyle paused, because this did not seem to be in keeping with Howard's nature; he wouldn't be so—so *selfish*. Instead, he was the type to be happy if Mary was happy. So, it should be presumed that Howard's warning wasn't to be taken lightly; there was a grave problem, here, that Doyle needed to address—and no shirking it just because it was crackin' awkward.

But—on the other hand—try as she might, Doyle was having a hard time believing that Savoie posed any danger to Mary—especially considering the way Savoie had treated the young widow ever since Howard's death—with such compassion, and outright kindness. It was very much out-of-character—although, that wasn't exactly fair; it was undeniable that Savoie had hidden depths—only see how he'd taken-in Emile, and now doted on the boy. A ghostly psychiatrist had once told her something about Savoie—she couldn't really remember, since it was all incomprehensible shrink-speak, but it was along the lines that Savoie saw himself in Emile, and wanted to right all the wrongs that he'd experienced when he was young.

I don't know what to do, Doyle admitted to herself, as she frowned into the computer screen. But it seems clear that I've got to do *something*, and so mayhap I will drop some hints to Mary when next we are at the park, together.

Closing the laptop, Doyle decided that she'd learned enough to help Acton with his interview, and—after listening to the nursery monitor's blessed silence for a few moments—she decided to call Nellie, to see what it was she wanted.

"Hallo, Nellie. Reynolds said you'd called."

"Yes, Kathleen, and I know you are busy, so I will get straight to the point. I hope you don't think I'm over-reacting, but I am very worried about Mrs. Rossa."

Doyle raised her brows; St. Michael's had hired a new bookkeeper in recent months. "Oh? Is she stealin' pennies, from the offerin' plate?"

"Oh, no—nothing like that. But she didn't come in to work

yesterday or today, and I am worried about her. I don't think she has any family, in the area, and so I don't know who to ask."

Surprised, Doyle offered, "She must be hangin' about with my new nanny, then. She's done a bunk, too."

"Has she? But I am a little concerned—I don't think Mrs. Rossa would be so unreliable, and I am worried that she has come to harm."

Doyle suggested, "Does she have a contact, on her employment form?"

"I've called, but it is a disconnected number."

"Have you checked the hospitals?"

"They won't tell me anything, because I am not a relative."

"Ah," said Doyle, as the penny dropped. "Lucky, it is, that you know someone in law enforcement."

"I didn't want to impose, Kathleen, but if you wouldn't mind—"

"No trouble a'tall. Give me her full name—and a description, too, in the event she's got amnesia or somethin'."

A description was actually more pertinent to check against any Jane Does at the morgue, but no need to alarm Nellie unnecessarily; the general population would be very surprised to hear how many unidentified corpses tended to pile up in the London morgue.

"Thank you so much."

"I'll call you back, as soon as I check."

Doyle rang off, and duly pulled-up the general database again so as to run the bookkeeper's name on a "whereabouts" check. Nothing. She'd used her credit card and mobile two days ago, but nothing since then.

Which wasn't a good sign—it almost never was, when a person suddenly stopped making payments or using their electronics. Doyle then pulled up the morgue records, and began matching Jane Doe descriptions. There—a possible match presented itself; having come in two days before, and with the same general age and description.

With grim resignation, she phoned Nellie again. "I'm afraid it doesn't look good, Nellie. There's a possible match in the morgue, and Mrs. Rossa stopped usin' her credit cards and phone about the same time."

"Oh—oh, no," the other woman exclaimed. "I'll go, to see if it is her. If she has no one else, we will see her buried, with a funeral."

Doyle did a quick review of her busy day tomorrow, and weighed adding yet another task against her uncertain childcare situation. "Can we do it late afternoon, tomorrow? I'm doin' a field interview with Williams, and I'll have him drop me off at the church."

"Thank you, Kathleen," said Nellie. "I will pray that we hear from Mrs. Rossa, before then."

"Here's hopin'," Doyle agreed, and tried to sound more optimistic than she felt.

CHAPTER 19

*T*hat night, Doyle lay with her husband in their bed, cooling down after yet another heated session of lovemaking. "It's the pasta," Doyle pronounced. "I can see the benefits, already."

"It was very good," he agreed, although he wasn't enthusiastic, because he wasn't much for pasta.

"Well, brace yourself, because I'm on a mission to fatten you up, and Reynolds knows his way around a kitchen. Faith, it seems as though everyone else does, save me."

"And me," he pointed out.

"And you," she agreed, and reached to kiss his shoulder. "We aren't a good pairin', really, because neither one of us can boil water, and we'd never survive in the wilderness."

"We could always forage," he suggested.

"Of course we could."

He turned to throw a fond arm over her, and pull her close. "It means to gather food from whatever is at hand."

She made a wry mouth. "Only if we were tryin' to survive in an apple orchard, I think."

He smiled. "Perhaps."

"Hence," she said, wisely. "And, here's a wrinkle; Miss Valerie never showed up, today, and we can't raise her."

He made a small sound of annoyance. "Is that so?"

"It is, indeed. I was reluctant to squeak on her with the agency, but if she doesn't show tomorrow I think we've no choice."

He seemed more amused, than anything else. "So, Edward won?"

"Leave it to you, to think of it in those terms, my friend. We can't allow a boyo his age to think he calls the shots around here, which is one of the reasons I'm hopin' this was just some sort of mix-up, and she'll turn up again."

Idly, he intertwined her fingers in his. "Should we do a 'whereabouts' check?"

"Funny you should ask—I just did one, for Nellie's new bookkeeper. But she had no relatives in the area, and Miss Valerie definitely does. If she's had an accident or somethin' we'd have heard about it—so it's much more likely that there's been some sort of mix-up. She's not one who'd snub the likes of you, after all —not if she wants to keep workin' for the nobs."

"Very true," he agreed.

"We'll give it one more day, then we'll call the agency. Callie's slated to come over tomorrow to help with Tommy, which means I'm goin' to be doin' my rounds like a county nurse to get everythin' I need done in one day."

He raised his brows. "What do you need done?"

She held up her fingers to count off. "In the mornin' I've your interview, then after the boys go down to nap, I'm assistin' Williams on a follow-up call, and then—last but not least—I'm takin' Nellie over to the morgue because I've a bad feelin' that one of the Jane Does is her poor bookkeeper."

This was of interest, and he asked, "Foul play?"

"Don't know, as yet."

"What is your follow-up, with Williams?"

Doyle had been half-hoping that he wouldn't ask—a fond hope, since this was Acton, after all—and so she explained. "We're headed over to Griffin Transport Company. I wanted to have another look 'round, to make sure there aren't any overlooked perps still hauntin' the halls."

She could sense him relax, which was interesting; apparently, he'd been worried that she was going to go nose around somewhere he'd rather she didn't.

Thoughtfully, he suggested, "Check to see if anyone left their employ within the pertinent time frame."

"Aye, aye, sir," she teased.

He lifted her hand, to kiss it. "Not that it wouldn't occur to you."

"I will gladly take any and all advice, my friend. I've no ego about it, whatsoever."

Her scalp started prickling, and she paused. What? she thought in surprise; whose ego is mucking things up?

But her husband was already on to the next topic. "The Denisovich interview is scheduled for nine."

"Are we playin' him as a suspect?"

This referred to interrogation techniques; oftentimes, police would hide the fact they thought the witness a likely suspect so as to encourage him to relax his guard. An equally effective technique was to encourage him to believe he was about to be hauled away in leg irons, and Acton was very good at deciding which technique was most likely to win the day.

"I think we've no choice but to play him as a suspect; he's no

fool, and must know that the situation does not look good for
him."

This was of interest, and Doyle turned her head toward him.
"D'you truly think he may have done it? It's a bit hard to believe,
that he'd wait so long to take his revenge on his wayward wife. Or
that he'd make it quite so obvious."

"We will see," he replied, which was very much in keeping;
Acton tended to analyze the evidence as it was presented, whilst
Doyle was more of a leaper-to-conclusions. She was firmly
convinced that this was why they worked so well, together; the
solving of crimes often took a little of both.

Idly, she rubbed his chest with her palm. "Will Sir Vikili be
there?"

"I have not heard from him, either way."

"Mayhap he's sick to the back teeth of givin' you the head's
up, and he's goin' to take a day off."

He picked up her hand, and began to play with her fingers. "I
took a longer look at Nazy's Kian, today."

She shifted her head, to look at him. "And?"

"He is related to Sir Vikili—a distant cousin. I imagine that is
how he obtained his current position—Denisovich bought
Howard's building, and Sir Vikili probably put forward one of his
relatives for a job."

Doyle considered this with a slight frown. "Strange, then, that
Sir Vikili wanted to drop a warnin' about our Kian—although I
suppose that would explain why he didn't want to be seen as
doin' so."

"Stranger still, there is nothing I can find to set off any alarms.
Kian went to a good school—good grades. This would appear to
be his first job."

Doyle raised her brows. "A bit of a surprise, that is; that
someone with his connections would be jobbin' it, like us lesser

beings." She eyed him. "Although I suppose I can only speak for myself. Did you ever have a job?"

"I have a job, now," he pointed out, a bit defensively.

"I mean a job-job, like the fish-market."

"Sad to say, I did not."

"Knock me down with a feather," she declared. "Although it would have been better than a raree-show, to see the likes of you dealin' with the fishmongers."

"More likely, I would have wanted to deal with you."

She rewarded this thought with a fond kiss on his shoulder. "We would have lived in a snug cottage by the sea, and kept any and all servants to a minimum."

"That does sound ideal," he lied, and she chuckled.

With some regret, Doyle moved on from sweet-talking with her husband and came back to the topic at hand. "Sir Vikili wouldn't have gone to the trouble, if there wasn't somethin' dodgy about Kian. Passin' along vague warnings is not his style, at all."

"I would agree."

She suggested, "Mayhap I should meet with the boyo—strike up a conversation, and see if I can catch a sense."

"A good idea," he agreed.

"If he's at the security desk, I can make-up a tale about having lost somethin'." She added, "Not tomorrow, though; my plate's already full."

"Yes; you mustn't overextend yourself, Kathleen."

"Not to mention I've no child-care, even if I wanted to overextend." Reminded, she asked, "Remember Mrs. Mackey, from The Mermaid Inn?"

"I do."

"What do we know about her?"

This caught his interest, and he turned his head to her. "Why?"

She knit her brow. "I don't know why. I may just have my wires crossed."

"I did vet her thoroughly."

"Well, you need more pasta then, because you also vetted Nazy's beau and apparently you missed the boat."

"Is there a concern?"

"Reynolds saw Mrs. Mackey at the park, today—she's visitin' town, on holiday. She kept mixin' up her supposed children when she spoke with me, but Reynolds had the impression there were no children a'tall."

Acton offered, "I would tend to agree with Reynolds. Her surname is actually Macagonova—she immigrated from western Russia, some years ago. I didn't see any indication she'd married, and so perhaps she concocted children so as to reassure you that she was capable when she handled ours."

"That could be it," Doyle agreed. "But it does seem odd, that she's popped up again, like a jack o' the clock. Although I think she's truly fond of Mary and her girls—we can't hold a candle."

"Edward did give her a scare," he noted, fairly.

"And a broken drainpipe. Faith, that boyo is fearless; I'll be more grey than red, before he gets to kindergarten."

"I think your hair is more properly auburn," he corrected, as he ran a fond hand through it. "A beautiful color; it was the first thing I noticed."

Smiling, she rolled over so as to nestle her back into his chest. "It's lucky I've got this mop, then; it made me stand-out from the crowd, when you were lookin' down from your window. Just think of where you'd be today, if some blonde floozy had caught your eye instead."

"Many have tried; all have failed."

She laughed. "Well, don't count me amongst the 'tryin'. More like I was wanderin' about blindly, like a hooded goose."

"It was a dilemma." He began to press kisses along her nape. "All I needed was the slightest encouragement."

"You were too fearsome," she admitted. "Scared the dickens out of me."

"Stronger measures were necessary." Gently, he pulled her over, and began to kiss her in earnest.

"Rushed me to the altar, and then threw me into bed." With a happy sigh, she twined her arms around his neck. "And here we are."

"A very successful strategy," he murmured.

Chuckling, she broke away for a moment to point out, "We're not goin' to make any progress, Michael, if you keep burnin' off all the calories that I'm stuffin' into you."

But she was to be given no response, as instead he rather firmly pressed her into the soft bed.

Nothin' for it, she decided; the man's got the bit between his teeth.

CHAPTER 20

*T*hat night, the ghostly spectre of Nigel Howard visited Doyle again.

"I keep gettin' distracted, from this vengeance-business," she apologized. "I was goin' to try and winkle-out more information but then I fell asleep." Thinking to gloss over any explanations that involved raging-sex and re-awakened hormones, she concluded, "I'm that sorry."

"Not at all," the ghost assured her. "You are doing very well."

This was a surprise, and Doyle offered doubtfully, "Truly? Well, from my end, it doesn't feel as though I'm makin' much progress—although I did find out that there's an independent actor who hasn't been rolled-up. And I think the reason he doesn't want me to find out about it, is because the person is slated to sink from sight—that's how he tends to handle such things, unfortunately."

"Vengeance," pronounced the ghost.

"More like wrath," she reminded him. "He's that wrathful—

even though he's tryin' to hide it from me, beneath all his soft-talk. It's eatin' him up."

"Yes. He has the bit between his teeth."

Doyle blinked in surprise. "Funny you should say that—that's just what I was thinkin'. He's doesn't want to be swayed, least of all by me."

"Wrath tends to cloud one's judgment," the ghost agreed.

Thoughtfully, she nodded. "We see that a lot, in our business. It's a huge problem—that people nurse their grievances, and are always plottin' revenge, back and forth, tit-for-tat. It's a never-endin' cycle."

"Exactly. There's good reason he doesn't want you there."

Puzzled, she frowned, slightly. "Who doesn't want me where?"

The ghost smiled. "You might say the fox is laying the trap for the gingerbread man."

There was a small, surprised silence, and then Doyle ventured, "I think you're mixed-up, Mr. Howard; it was the last ghost who went on-and-on about the nursery story. You're the ghost who speaks of that other story—the Greek one, with those two famous fighters." With a mighty effort, Doyle managed to dredge up their names. "Hector, and—and Achilles."

"That story is very similar to the nursery story, actually."

With some confusion, Doyle admitted, "I'm not seein' it, I guess."

"Don't worry," he soothed with gentle encouragement. "You will."

Doyle decided she may as well mention, "Acton thinks your dog's name was 'Raven'."

"Yes," the ghost agreed, with a fond smile. "A good fellow."

With all patience, Doyle persisted, "Then, who's 'Hector'?"

"Oh, Hector's very loyal. And rather ferocious; the best sort of watch-dog."

There was another small silence, and Doyle slowly shook her head. "None of this makes a sliver of sense to me—there's far too many things to keep track of. I can't sort-out what's important, and what's not."

But the ghost only tilted his head, as he regarded her kindly.

"It's *all* important?" she asked in surprise. "For heaven's sake —how can all of these things be related? Next, you'll be speakin' of bread-puddin' again."

"I did love Mary's bread-pudding," he teased.

"Well, it's a shame that Acton doesn't like bread-puddin'; that would fatten him up in a trice."

"It wouldn't matter," the ghost explained, serious again. "He doesn't want to be soothed."

With some concern, she ventured, "Then, what am I supposed to do? He's got the bit between his teeth."

"Avenge my death," the ghost instructed, and then—in an instant—he was gone.

CHAPTER 21

The next morning, Doyle sat with baby Tommy at the breakfast table—alone for a few minutes, since Callie had taken Edward to get dressed, and Acton was down in his office making phone calls before they left for their interview.

She'd been mulling over what the ghost had said, and—in her mind, at least—two things seemed to stand out—although there may be more, when she had more time to think it over.

The first was the ghost had implied that all the strange happenings that seemed to pop up every time she turned around were somehow related. The second, was he'd made a reference to the gingerbread man.

This seemed significant; the last ghost she'd dealt with—Bill Blakney—had also referred to the nursery story, even though it was hard to imagine two men who were more different. Blakney had been Mary's first husband—a rough, tattooed fellow, who'd participated in the guns-smuggling rig by way of his pawn shop. Howard, by contrast, was Mary's second husband, and he was one of those posh-types that you'd see haunting the West End restaurants; over-polite, and the complete opposite of rough-and-tattooed. Faith, if you threw Savoie into the mix, it just went to show that Mary had—elcletic? Was that the word?—taste, when it came to men.

So; why would both these ghosts mention the nursery story? And especially when there seemed to be no rhyme nor reason—save that they'd both stood as stepfather to Gemma, and Gemma had liked the story when she was littler. Edward had been obsessed with it, and Gemma would listen along, too.

Gazing out the picture windows, Doyle tried to make sense of it—what was the connection? Blakney had been killed—just like Howard was—but Blakney's death had been collateral damage in the original corruption rig that Howard had uncovered. Blakney had been murdered in an attempt to blackmail poor Williams—which brought up yet another connection to Mary. But Blakney's death had no connection to Howard's, did it? They were separated by time, and motive, and perpetrators.

So, mayhap she had it by the wrong leg; mayhap it wasn't about the two men and what they had or didn't have in common, but it was the nursery story itself that was significant. *Run, run, fast as you can; you can't catch me, I'm the gingerbread man.* The gingerbread man had been sadly mistaken, of course; the fox had out-foxed him in the end, and eaten him up.

When Blakney had spoken of the tale, he'd implied that Philippe Savoie was the gingerbread man—Savoie had been his gov in the smuggling rig, and Blakney had mightily admired the Frenchman. He'd admired Savoie for being so slippery, and it had been left to the fair Doyle to explain to Blakney that the gingerbread man had actually come to a bad end, much to the ghost's surprise and disbelief.

And now, Howard was saying that the other story—that ancient one, that went on-and-on about the stupid Greeks—was very similar to the nursery story. Which may or may not be true, and since Doyle was not one who was inclined to study ancient treatises, she went to the next best thing.

"Reynolds," she called out to the butler. "Remember that story we spoke about—the story about the two warriors?"

Reynolds paused, in his washing-up duties. "*Troilus and Cressida*, madam?"

She eyed him. "Not a clue, what you just said."

"Hector and Achilles," he amended.

"That's the one. Did either one of them outfox the other?"

"Yes, madam. Achilles outfoxed Hector."

Doyle brightened. "Excellent, Reynolds—*now* we're gettin' somewhere. Give me the short version, if you please."

The servant gathered his thoughts, and then recited, "Hector had killed Achilles' friend, and so Achilles swore revenge. The two men met in combat, with Hector wearing Achilles' stolen armor. Achilles speared him in a gap that existed between the armor and the neck; because Hector was wearing Achilles' stolen armor, he knew where there was a weakness."

"Faith, but there's a comeuppance," Doyle mused. "Good one, Achilles."

The servant added, "To be fair, madam, the point of the story is rather a cautionary one. Achilles was just as prideful and vengeful as Hector, and each man eventually paid for it with his life."

"Is that so? Well, it only goes to show you that Isaac was miles wiser," she decided thoughtfully.

Reynolds frowned, slightly. "I do not believe there was an 'Isaac' in the story, madam."

She smiled. "There was an 'Isaac' in the only story that truly matters, my friend. Isaac knew that vengeance was a tangle-patch and should be avoided at all costs." She paused, remembering what the ghost had said. "Vengeance is a form of wrath, after all, and wrath is one of the seven deadly sins."

"Quite so, madam," said the servant, who knew better than to delve into religious matters with the lady of the house.

At this point, Acton emerged from the stairway. "Are we ready?"

"We are," she answered as she rose, and walked over to settle the baby on the sofa. "I just topped Tommy off, and so he should be good for Callie till we're back."

"Very good."

Reynolds had gone to fetch their coats from the hall closet, and —as she slid her arms through the sleeves—Doyle observed thoughtfully, "So; Hector is the gingerbread man and Achilles is the fox."

"In a manner of speaking, madam." This, said in the diplomatic tone of one who wouldn't necessarily agree with such an abbreviated synopsis.

Acton smiled, as he adjusted Doyle's scarf, tucking it into the collar of her coat. "What's this?"

"Just thinkin' out loud. There's common themes, you know, runnin' through famous stories."

"I cannot disagree."

"Backwards-speak," Doyle pronounced. "You must be feelin' better."

"I was not aware that I was unwell," he protested in some amusement.

"And there's even more backwards-speak, heaped upon the last. Good one, Reynolds—mayhap you could bake him a cake today; we won't be able to understand him a'tall, by the morrow."

"Very good, madam," said the butler. "Do you have a preference, sir?"

Acton accepted his valise from the servant's hand. "Not Rasputin's honey-cakes."

"Certainly not, sir." Reynolds unbent enough to offer a small smile.

Posh-people humor, thought Doyle, as she made a mighty effort not to roll her eyes; give me a straightforward pub-joke any day. But then she found that she was distracted, as she accompanied her husband out the door, because her scalp had started prickling.

CHAPTER 22

They'd arrived at Denisovich's offices, which were overly-elegant, and with a lot of gilt covering the picture frames and the furniture. His Assistant—a sleek, slender young man—greeted them, and explained that he'd inform Mr. Denisovich they had arrived.

He suggested they take a seat, but Acton never sat whilst waiting for someone, because that would not be in keeping with the pecking-order. Instead, he'd remain standing in the middle of the reception room, so that everyone was made aware of this fact.

Whilst they waited, Doyle whispered to her husband, "Tell me about Rasputin's honey-cakes."

"They were poisoned," her husband whispered back.

"Oh," she said.

I must have got my wires crossed, she decided; no way, no how, is Reynolds going to poison Acton—he would consider it a crime against nature and crackin' impolite, besides.

The Assistant returned to usher them into the spacious office, which gave-off the impression of being rather cluttered, despite the fact that everything within it was of the finest quality. Doyle was not at all surprised to see that Sir Vikili was standing by the windows.

"Sir Vikili," said Acton, coming forward and politely offering his hand.

"Chief Inspector," said the other man, taking it with equal politeness.

And here we go, thought Doyle, trying to tamp down her alarm.

They then greeted Denisovich, who looked a bit older and rougher 'round the edges than his bio picture. His expression was impassive, but Doyle knew that the man was very, very wary—as well he should be, what with a murdered ex-wife and a brace of Scotland Yard's finest darkening his door. But—rather surprisingly—when she took his hand, she'd the sudden sense of something else—something unfathomably sad. He was steeped in misery, was Mr. Denisovich, and he was that bleak; as though the universe had come crashing down around his head and he was using all his powers just to stay upright.

Well, here's a wrinkle, she thought in surprise; our Mr. Denisovich isn't half so tough as he looks.

They were seated, and—like a good support officer—Doyle duly removed her pad and pencil from her rucksack as she prepared to take notes.

Acton began, "As I imagine you are aware, we would like to ask a few questions in connection with the recent death of Ms. Lanska."

"Of course," the Russian man replied, with a nod.

"If you would, please describe your relationship with your ex-wife."

This was an indication that Acton was going to take the long route; if they were needing only to have the crucial question answered, he'd have headed in that direction immediately. So; there was something else here that her husband wished to explore. It would also put Sir Vikili at a disadvantage; it was much easier to caution a client when he was answering direct questions than when he was giving a recitation.

The witness gave out a short bark of laughter, and spread his hands. "Where to start?"

Acton smiled slightly. "Why did you divorce?"

The man heaved a sigh. "She was a bad woman, Chief Inspector. Loose morals—she had no respect for me."

Doyle casually lifted a hand to brush her hair from her forehead, which was the signal she used to let Acton know that the witness was lying.

Acton noted, "Nonetheless, you were required to pay her an impressive amount of alimony every month. It must have rankled."

Denisovich shrugged. "I am a rich man, Chief Inspector. I am not going to kill her just to save money."

This was true, and Doyle kept her hands in her lap.

This seemed a good opening, and Acton decided to take it. "You had nothing to do with her death?"

The man shook his head, adamantly. "No."

Doyle kept her hands in her lap. So much for the vengeful ex-husband theory.

But Acton was not one to fold his tent if there was more information to be gained—after all, *someone* had killed Sasha Lanska, and this fellow might know more than he was letting on. "She belonged to the Mossovet at one time, I believe."

Denisovich made a derisive sound. "She was a Bolshevik —always."

Sir Vikili, who'd been listening without comment, shifted

slightly in his chair, as though he was contemplating an objection to this line of questioning.

Doyle knew that Acton had noticed the movement too, because his next question pursued the subject more pointedly. "She was a Bolshevik, and yet she married a rich man?"

Sir Vikili interjected, "The reasons for the marriage are irrelevant, Chief Inspector."

Acton kept his gaze on the witness. "If you would answer the question, please."

The witness sighed, hugely. "Yes, she married a rich man. And even after we divorced, she still took much of my money, every month." He spread his hands again. "She was an actress, Chief Inspector—and Russian. It was all for show—to get good publicity from the press, here. They are in love with the Bolsheviks."

Doyle brushed her hair off her forehead.

"Did she have any enemies, in St. Petersburg?"

"No—she left all that behind her."

Doyle scribbled a note, which was their signal when there were multiple untruths in a row, and the hair-brushing would seem overdone. After all, Sir Vikili was watching, and Sir Vikili was no fool—not that anyone would guess that she was a human truth-detector, of course, but his suspicions might be aroused if she were seen to be giving constant hand-signals.

Acton paused for a significant moment, and then asked, "Left 'all' what, behind her?"

Sir Vikili cautioned, "I don't see how this is relevant, Chief Inspector."

For the first time, Acton rested his thoughtful gaze on the solicitor. "There may be echoes from the past in this victim's murder. It has come to my attention that she was associated with several Watch-List subjects, all of whom originated from St.

Petersburg. Indeed, the manner of her murder speaks of a rather brutal message."

Sir Vikili did not respond, but nodded in acquiescence toward his client.

Doyle could sense a flare of alarm as the witness fashioned his answer; so—he regretted his remark, and immediately began to backtrack. "I did not mean to imply anything about enemies from the old days. Instead, I meant that she was going through rich men, even when she was young."

Doyle scribbled more pretend-notes.

Acton regarded him in silence for a moment. "Do you know of anyone, who might wish her dead? Did you have any suspicions, when you heard the news?"

"No," he replied, and Doyle returned her hand to her lap because—rather surprisingly—this was true. This witness was awash in secrets, but he'd been genuinely shocked by his ex-wife's death.

Denisovich glanced out the window, briefly, and Doyle could sense that he was making a mighty effort to retain control of his emotions. "She was—she was an amazing woman, despite our troubles. I was very sorry to hear of it."

But Acton was not one to wax sentimental. "I believe you are the principal officer in the limited company which owned the subject yachts."

The man glanced toward Sir Vikili, who nodded—no point in trying to withhold information that was on public record. "This is true."

"Will insurance cover the property loss?"

The witness sighed. "No, because the authorities have concluded that it was arson." He paused, and made a sound of regret. "My beautiful boats."

"A coin shop in Bristol was also burned in an arson fire, at approximately the same time. I believe you held an ownership interest in that business, also."

There was a sudden, subtle shift in the atmosphere, and Doyle hid her surprise. Not only did Acton know about the coin shop fire, it seemed clear that he thought it was related to this one—which would only made sense, after all, and would explain why the local investigators immediately decided there might be a Public Accounts case connection. It couldn't be a coincidence, that two pass-throughs for the money-laundering scheme had burnt down, at almost the exact same time.

"Yes, I am an owner," Denisovich warily agreed.

Doyle remembered that Savoie was an owner, too—at least, that was what Mary had said. It was unlikely, however, that the illustrious Chief Inspector would bring up that little subject, being as any road that led to Savoie could also lead to him.

Acton continued, "And your bakery, here in town, has also been torched. I might be forgiven for thinking that it looks as though someone is attempting to destroy evidence."

"Don't answer," instructed Sir Vikili.

Acton let it go, and continued, "Will insurance cover these other losses—the coin shop, and the bakery?"

Denisovich sighed. "No. But the Frenchman tells me he will buy-out my interest in the bakery."

There was a pause. "'The Frenchman' being—"

"Savoie," the man said, as though stating the obvious.

Acton nodded, and Doyle caught his leap of surprise. Whatever her husband knew about this trail of arson fires—and it seemed clear that he knew more than he was saying—he didn't know that Savoie was looking to buy-out his partner's interest in the burnt-up bakery.

And so, his next question—for a change—was out of genuine curiosity. "Why does Savoie seek to buy you out?"

Again, the man shrugged. "I do not know. You do not ask the Frenchman why he does things."

Acton was silent, and the silence stretched out for a few long moments. This was an interrogation technique that was often useful, because witnesses—for whatever reason—tended to fill any silences by talking too much. Denisovich, however, seemed well-used to parrying law enforcement inquiries, and so he was not going to volunteer any further information about the bakery fire.

Doyle bent her head, trying to make sense what they'd learned. The obvious implication was what Acton had pointed out —evidence was being destroyed. But if this fellow was involved in the other fires, that made for a bit of a puzzle, since he wasn't the one who'd set the yacht-fire. Mayhap he panicked, after the yachts were burned—worried about the scrutiny that would be turned his way? But he didn't seem the panicking type, not to mention that the other two fires would only draw more scrutiny toward him.

And—lest we forget—Acton hadn't wanted the fair Doyle to know about this man's involvement, in the first place. She'd had to put on her detective-hat, and sweet-talk Nazy, in order to garner the information. But now—now, Acton had decided he needed a truth-detector, because—even though he was trying to keep the wife of his bosom in the dark—there was something here that he didn't understand.

And—most tellingly—Acton hadn't asked the witness an obvious question—whether he'd set the other two fires, or knew who did. Which meant, it seemed, that Acton already knew, and didn't want his support officer to get any bright ideas.

This line of troubling thought was interrupted when Acton broke his silence by asking the witness, "I understand your Assistant was employed at the bakery for a time."

Oh-ho, thought Doyle, as she caught the man's suppressed flare of acute alarm. Now, isn't *that* a little item of interest?

"My nephew, Rolph," the witness replied, with a monumental effort to sound off-hand. "I promise you, Chief Inspector; he knows nothing of any of this."

"We will interview him, nonetheless. He may have noticed something, unaware of its importance."

There was a small, tense pause. "Certainly," the witness replied.

CHAPTER 23

*R*olph-the-assistant was duly called-in, and Acton explained that he was investigating an arson fire at the young man's former place of employment.

That's interesting, thought Doyle as she sat with her poised pencil; usually witnesses were not interviewed together, but Acton doesn't mind that Denisovich was listening-in.

"I don't know as I can help, much," the Assistant replied, with a casual shrug. "I didn't work there very long—I didn't like the early hours."

"Was the business profitable?"

Again, the fellow shrugged. "I wouldn't know—I worked delivery, and I wasn't allowed anywhere near the books."

Doyle brushed her hair from her forehead, and thought, he's a bit brash, and thinks he can outsmart Acton. Which Acton, of course, allows him to believe even though Acton eats his type for breakfast and on a regular basis. Nothing like a witness who's full of himself, to give a detective too much information; it would be far better for our Rolph to take a leaf from Denisovich, here, and button your lip when Acton comes calling.

"Did you know of any employees who were let go, during the time you were there?"

The young man smirked slightly. "The Frenchman did a purge a few months in. He didn't consult with me, so I don't know his reasons."

Politely, Acton asked, "'The Frenchman' being—?"

"Oh—a chap named Philippe Savoie. He was one of the owners—he tended to be a bit tight on the reins."

And the other two men are mightily wishing that this fellow would snabble it, Doyle thought; in fact, I think Acton's using him to needle them, a bit, which is interesting.

In the same polite tone, Acton asked, "Did you ever speak with Mr. Savoie?"

The young man shrugged, negligently. "No. He couldn't fire me, so I just avoided being around him."

Acton lifted his brows. "I see. Why couldn't you be fired?"'

The witness explained, almost kindly, "Mr. Denisovich, here, got me the job and he was one of the owners."

Acton nodded. "I see. Your good fortune, then."

"It pays to have connections," the young man agreed, and his knowing gaze slid over to rest on Doyle for a moment.

Oh-oh, thought Doyle. Katy bar the door.

But Acton appeared not to notice the insinuation, and instead asked, "Is it possible that one of the purged employees may have set the fire? Did you catch a sense, that one of them could be capable?"

With a sudden, calculating expression, the young man offered, "Rory Flynn. He seemed capable to me."

Fah—here's a nasty fellow, thought Doyle, as she scribbled a note to show he was lying; he's very much enjoying the idea of setting the police on someone that he didn't like.

Acton nodded, his attitude one of gratitude for such a promising lead. "Would you know the names of any of the other employees who were involved in the purge?"

The young man shrugged, yet again—this time with a trace of impatience. "No."

Doyle scribbled a note.

Acton nodded. "No matter; their names will be in the records, certainly."

"Unless the records were burned-up," the fellow pointed out, since the Chief Inspector seemed to have overlooked this pertinent fact.

"Of course," Acton conceded. "We must hope that such is not the case."

"I do think the fire started in the office area," the witness warned.

"Did it? That does not bode well," Acton conceded.

"Exactly."

He's one of those who always has to have the last word, thought Doyle; and he's too puffed-up to think that mayhap he should mind himself, for once.

"Thank you; you have been very helpful," said Acton without a trace of irony. Please; take my card, and do not hesitate to contact me if you can think of any other information that might be of interest."

The young man smirked a bit more as he accepted the card graciously, wholly unaware that the other two men in the room were very much dismayed by Acton's polite manner.

CHAPTER 24

They took their leave, and Doyle stayed quiet as she and Acton exited the posh office building and then made their way down the street, toward the Range Rover. Her husband was deep in thought, and so Doyle patiently waited for him to ask for a report, like a good and respectful support officer. Her thoughts, however, were less than good and respectful toward her senior command, being as she was mighty tired of always having to include him in her list of suspects.

And there were several good reasons to do so. First and foremost, Acton knew his way around an arson fire—a nasty habit, but there it was—and second, there'd been an odd little nuance, between the three men, when they were talking about the other two fires; as though they all had a shared knowledge that they didn't wish to speak aloud.

And—most tellingly—Acton had never asked Denisovich if he'd set the other two fires, or if he suspected who might be behind them. Therefore, one could not discard the sad fact that it may have been the illustrious Chief Inspector, himself, who was behind them. She knew that Acton hadn't torched the yachts—since it had been the truth, when he'd told her he wasn't involved—but as for the coin shop and the bakery, all bets were off, and it would certainly explain Denisovich's confused wariness.

But—on the other hand—she could sense that her husband was genuinely frustrated as they approached the car, which would surely point to the hopeful fact that he hadn't been involved? It was all very puzzling, and she almost felt sorry for him—trying to find out the truth about something without tipping-off his wedded wife as to exactly what it was.

I think he's sincerely trying to find out who's killed Sasha, she decided; and so he needed me there, to help him rule-out the ex-husband. But then he didn't want to dwell on the details about the fires, for fear I'd catch him out in something.

"What was your impression?"

Recalled to her duties, Doyle readily replied, "Denisovich is that wary of you—and knows more than he's sayin'—but mainly, he's grievin' Sasha. He's devastated that she's dead, Michael. I think he still loves her very much, but he can't let on." She paused. "It's rather sad."

Her husband raised his brows, as he opened her car door. "That is very interesting."

"'Tis," she agreed. "It's not a'tall in keepin' with what's been said about them." She waited until he come around and got in the car, to add, "And he was very unhappy when you handed his puffed-up Assistant your card. He knows the fellow's a weak link."

Acton smiled slightly, as he guided the car out into traffic. "The Assistant is their mutual son—Denisovich and Sasha's."

She stared at him in astonishment—trust Acton, to know all the juicy secrets. "So; not his nephew? I wonder why the charade?"

"Sasha was an actress, and famous for her love-affairs. It may be that she didn't want it generally known she'd a grown son."

"Mayhap," Doyle agreed. "And mayhap the son resents the charade; he's definitely not mournin' his dead mum—not like our Mr. Denisovich."

As they paused at a traffic light, her husband noted, "I can find no indication that Denisovich and his ex-wife were in communication after they divorced."

But Doyle could only shake her head. "I'd be very much surprised if they weren't communicatin', Michael. His grief feels— it feels sharp; not like it would for someone you'd loved from years ago."

Acton noted, "He did have a Javid, in his office. It looked to be a portrait of Sasha."

She stared at him in surprise; trust Acton, to notice the details. "Good catch, Michael." Javid was a famous artist—she'd once painted Doyle's portrait, as a matter of fact—but more to the point, she was Sir Vikili's betrothed. "D'you think that Sir Vikili may have acted as a go-between for Sasha and Denisovich? It would only make sense—he was the man's solicitor. But then, why all the secrecy? It's not as though either one of them has remarried."

"A very good question."

Thinking this over, she gazed out the windscreen for a moment. "When did they divorce—about how long ago?"

"A little over three years."

Doyle mused, "Mayhap we should look into what happened, three years ago. Mayhap there was a threat of some sort that made them pretend to split-up. Or it was a tactical divorce—they divorced for financial reasons. If he's payin' a huge alimony, the divorce may have been set-up to transfer his assets away from a creditor."

He nodded. "Which would further support the premise that he wasn't involved in his ex-wife's death."

"Her death is the last thing he wanted," Doyle said with complete certainty. "Mark me."

He went silent again, and she reviewed the scenery passing outside her window as she thought about this—about how Acton was keen about Sasha's murder and the reasons for it, but was not so very keen about the two other arson fires.

She decided that she may as well take the bull by the horns—sometimes, when she surprised Acton with a question, she could catch a sense. "They were both very wary—Denisovich and Sir Vikili—when you spoke of the coin-shop fire."

Acton replied, "As well they should be; these fires could very well pull Denisovich into the dock for the Public Accounts trial."

Doyle lifted her brows, seeing his point; Howard's murder trial would take priority, of course, but there would be a second criminal trial to address the Public Accounts embezzlement rig, which was separate and apart from the murder trial. "If they can pin these fires on Denisovich, it would present a possible case of accessory-after-the-fact. Whether or not he was involved in the Public Accounts rig, he's destroyed evidence."

"Yes."

She blew out a breath. "Small wonder, that Denisovich was nervous as a cat—and Sir Vikili, too; faith, the poor man's probably worried he'll have to cancel his weddin' plans, if the Public Accounts scandal blows up again."

Her husband made no response and seemed disinclined to discuss the matter further, which only caused Doyle to harbor a very familiar suspicion; after all, if this had been Acton's object all along—to tie-in Denisovich to the Public Accounts scandal—there would have been no harm in explaining this beforehand to the wife of his bosom. But instead, he treading very carefully—

and wasn't asking pertinent questions—so as to keep her in the dark.

And so, she took firm hold of the bull's horns yet again. "You are hidin' your cards from me, Michael, and I've a bad feelin' about it. Tell me straight-out that you didn't set these other fires, so as to frame-up our Mr. Denisovich."

He gave her a reproachful glance. "I did not. I was with you on holiday, remember?"

"You did a fair amount of wanderin' off, as I recall," she countered. But it was a huge relief; he'd told the truth, and so she'd one less worry, in her quest for Howard-vengeance.

With all seriousness, her husband added, "It is a delicate situation, Kathleen, and I am afraid there are some secrets I must keep."

This was also true, and it seemed to indicate that he was having to choose the lesser of various evils, which—unfortunately —was part of one's job, when one was a Chief Inspector.

She wondered, for a moment, if Sir Vikili could be the object of his concern. Acton had protected the famous solicitor in the past— over a little matter of murder, as a matter of fact. And Sir Vikili— who had a poker-face every bit as good as Acton's—had been actually very unsettled during the entire interview.

Exploring this thought, she offered aloud, "Remember how I wondered if Sir Vikili was tryin' to give you a warnin', when he showed-up at the Bristol morgue? I wonder if somethin' similar was happenin' with this interview. I got the impression that he was steerin' you, a bit; I know it sounds strange to say, but he seemed more focused on you than he was on his client."

"The comment about the Bolsheviks," Acton agreed. "Yes—it was as though he wanted attention to be drawn."

Doyle knit her brow. "Remind me who the Bolsheviks are, husband."

"The revolutionary party, in Russia. You might say the members of the Mossovet are a remnant of the original Bolsheviks."

"Oh." Reminded, she observed, "Seems a bit strange, that a Russian mafia-type would be married to a Russian revolutionary-type."

"Perhaps it was the true reason they were forced to divorce," he offered. "Denisovich's known-associates would not be happy with the press attention Sasha tended to attract."

"There's a good point," she agreed. "And it would explain why he's still in love with her, even though they split. Which reminds me, when he told you that she'd left her St. Petersburg past behind, it wasn't true—although, since her death seems to be an admonishment-murder, I suppose that's no surprise."

Acton nodded thoughtfully. "Anything else?"

"I'll let you know, if I can think of anythin'."

He pulled into the parking garage at headquarters, and remarked, "Your point about a tactical divorce is a good one. I will attempt to trace what happened to Sasha's alimony payments—where the money went, and if it was being laundered. And I should have another look at her known-associates, to see if there was anyone who originated from St. Petersburg."

It was the moment of truth, and Doyle decided she'd no choice but to mention, "And—along those lines—I'm afraid our Williams was a known-associate."

CHAPTER 25

*a*cton raised a surprised brow. "Is that so?"

"A few drinks, is all," she hurriedly explained. "And not recently. For heaven's sake, don't tell Lizzie."

He tilted his head. "I may have to ask him about it, though. Sasha may have been trying to glean information from him."

In some surprise, Doyle asked, "Information about what?"

"Whatever got her killed. It seems clear that she was involved in more than acting."

Doyle could only reluctantly agree. "It does seem that she crossed the wrong people—loads of anger, in her manner of death."

He glanced at her. "Which means the fact that she was attempting to cultivate Williams is something that I should not ignore."

She nodded, slowly. "Aye, that; you're right, and I'm that dim for not havin' thought of it, myself."

After a few moments of silence, she added, in a casual tone, "And speakin' of which, let me see if Williams is available to nip over to the transport company right now, before I go home for lunch. This interview didn't take as long as I thought it would, and it would save me a trip this afternoon."

Her husband replied, "Right; I will hold off contacting him until you've had a chance to give him warning."

Doyle winced at being so easily caught-out. "Sorry. I have to walk a thin line, here, and it's not as though he'd withhold evidence, Michael."

"I know. Williams is your friend—I understand."

I'm not sure he does, she thought, as she reached over to cover his hand in gratitude. Her husband wasn't one to have friends, but he'd move heaven and earth to protect her friends, and he'd already done so in the past. So—in a way—Acton had friends-by-marriage who fell under his cloak of protection. It was another testament to the amazing power of love; under ordinary circumstances, he wouldn't give two pins about any of them save that they were dear to her, and—for him—that was enough.

Her scalp started prickling, and she paused to raise her head in the act of scrolling for Williams' number. "I think—I think our Mr. Denisovich was a bit foolish, when it came to Sasha. It was why he stuck by her side when she was courtin' the press. He'd have much rather flown under the radar—skirtin' the law, and doin' his shady business dealings—but he loved her madly, and couldn't help but try and please her. And now she's suddenly dead, and he's left with all the problems she's caused but no Sasha, to make it all worthwhile."

"An interesting insight," he said thoughtfully.

She nodded. "You almost feel sorry for him; the last thing he wants is to have a bright light, shinin' into his private doings. He's a lot like Sir Vikili, in that; love came along and dropped an atom bomb on all his well-laid plans. It made him to do things he'd never have done, otherwise—not in a million years."

"I can relate," her husband observed, and lifted her hand to kiss its back.

"Aye; you're the poster-child for it," she agreed with a small smile. "The 'old' you would be laughin' at the 'new' you, and callin' you rude names."

"The 'new' me has nothing but pity for the 'old' me."

"That's very sweet, Michael, but I think the 'old' you still keeps you up a'nights." She skewed a meaningful glance over at him.

"A very astute observation," he agreed in a mild tone.

Recognizing a brick wall when she saw one, Doyle phoned Williams to re-set their plans, and then, after she rang off, noted, "I may have to pump some milk, before I go out in the field—I don't want to spring a leak before I get home to Tommy."

And so, Doyle took refuge in Acton's office for a few minutes, sitting across from him whilst he caught up on his calls and using the breast-pump as quietly as she was able. And here's another scenario, she thought with some amusement, that would have made the old Acton's eyes start clear out of their sockets.

When she was finished—it was a stop-gap measure only, and so she inserted an extra breast pad just to be safe—she bade goodbye to her husband and quietly closed the door behind her, smiling at Nazy, who was seated at her desk in the hallway.

The girl seemed a bit glum, and Doyle wondered if Acton had already dropped a word in her ear about her questionable beau. After deciding that she was too nosy not to ask, she said brightly, "How's your sweetheart, Nazy?"

"I don't know—I cannot contact him, Officer Doyle. I've left many messages." Reluctantly, the other girl admitted, "I even went by his work, but they haven't seen him, either."

Doyle raised her brows. "So; he's disappeared from the face of the earth? Mother a' Mercy, but there's a lot of that goin' around."

She paused, because this was indeed strange. People were disappearing—and all about the same time. Was it a coincidence? Although there was a ready reason for this one—Nazy's beau must have indeed been warned-off, and that was the reason he was playing least-in-sight. Although that wouldn't explain why he was absent from work. Mayhap he'd seen her coming in, and hid whilst his mates sent her off.

There; that was probably the answer—she shouldn't be over-fanciful, and start jumping at shadows. And besides, there was no link between the three people who'd disappeared—the nanny, the bookkeeper, and Nazy's beau. Other than they were people in Doyle's orbit, of course—but even that was a stretch, considering how she'd never even met the bookkeeper or Nazy's beau.

However, as she made her way down to the front pavement—Williams was already out in the field, and was going to swing by to pick her up—she couldn't shake the feeling that attention should be paid. And in the fair Doyle's experience, where there seemed to be a lot of strange and unconnected goings-on, her wedded husband tended to be in the thick of it.

She paused for a moment, teetering on the edge of turning 'round to confront him about these disappearances. With some reluctance, however, she decided against it, mainly because—based on her experiences of the past few days—he'd probably just fob her off with a weasel-answer, just like he'd done in the car.

Oh, she thought suddenly, as she paused in walking. Did he give me a weasel-answer in the car? Frowning, she tried to remember what he'd said to make her think this, but came up empty.

Heaving a mental sigh, she continued walking. So; she should follow-up on this too—these disappearances, on top of Howard's vengeance-quest of course—that was the most important thing, with his murder-trial, right around the corner, and she mustn't be distracted from it—despite the fact that the ghost, himself, seemed easily distracted—what with his rambling-on about bread-pudding and the gingerbread man. For someone who was dead, he certainly seemed to be fixated on baked goods.

With a friendly wave at the Desk Sergeant, Doyle emerged through the lobby doors to wait outside for Williams and try not to feel overwhelmed by all the odd little things that seemed to be happening, each one hard upon the next. It was a frustrating feeling, and one with which she was well-familiar; it was as though she could see all the spokes of the wheel, but not the hub, that held them all together. You'll get there, the ghost had said, but she wished she'd the least idea of where it was that she was going.

CHAPTER 26

*T*he PC who was stationed on the front pavement saluted as he opened Williams' passenger door for her, and Doyle smiled her thanks and then slid into the car. "I need to warn you," she said immediately, as soon as the door closed behind her.

Williams checked his mirror, and pulled away. "Warn me of what?"

"Acton's goin' to look into Sasha's known-associates, and I felt I'd no choice but to mention your meetings."

"*Kath*—," he groaned in disbelief.

"He's got good reason, Thomas; he's wonderin' if she was tryin' to prime you for information."

With some exasperation, he pointed out, "And you think I wouldn't have noticed, if that was the case? Give me some credit."

"Good point," she admitted. "Sorry; I thought I'd best come clean."

"I just don't want Lizzie to catch wind."

"Then you shouldn't be dallyin' with famous actresses," Doyle

145

retorted. "Faith, you're lucky your snap wasn't splashed across the tabloids."

"Lesson learned," he agreed.

"Not that you aren't a handsome thing, Thomas, but d'you think she may have had ulterior motives? What did she want to talk about?"

"Nothing in particular—I asked about her work, of course."

"Did she ask about Acton?" This would be a likely topic, if the woman were up to no good.

"Not a word." He paused, and then admitted, "She did ask about Lizzie."

"Sizin' up the competition," Doyle remarked, with a knowing air.

But he protested, "I didn't have that sense, Kath—I know when a woman's giving me the green light, and I didn't think she was."

"Then why was she speakin' of Lizzie, if she wasn't tryin' to scout-out the lay of the land?"

He shrugged. "I think she was just showing a friendly interest."

"Famous actresses aren't known for showin' a friendly interest in the wife who's at home," Doyle reminded him. Thoughtfully, she knit her brow. "Sasha's ex-husband's got ties to the Russian mafia. Could she have been winklin' for information on a case? Your Lizzie was helpin' out at Mary's flat, right around that time —it was just after Hannah was born. But I think the main point of Lizzie's helpin' the Howards was to allow Acton and Howard to pass information back and forth to each other, with no one the wiser."

"Yes," he admitted. "They were about to break the Public Accounts case, and Acton didn't want anything to be recorded on government electronics, for fear the players would catch wind. Lizzie acted as a go-between."

She glanced over at him. "Could that have been the reason that Sasha was catfishin' you about Lizzie? Mayhap she was tryin' to winkle-out what you knew about the evidence that Lizzie was passin' back and forth."

With a small frown, Williams slowly shook his head. "I honestly don't think so, Kath—there wasn't a hint of that, and I would have been immediately suspicious. Instead, she just wanted to talk about ordinary things—she teased me about whether Lizzie was a good cook, and what things she liked to bake for me."

Doyle blinked. "Truly? Faith, we always seem to be circlin' back to baked goods."

"I'll be the shape of a circle, if I'm not careful. Between Mary and Lizzie, I've got to watch it—I don't know who's the better baker, and don't tell my mother I said so."

"I can't hold a candle," Doyle admitted. "I'd burn the corn flakes."

They drove in silence for a few minutes, and then he asked, "What's happened, that made Acton want to look into Sasha's known-associates?"

"We interviewed her ex-husband this mornin'—Denisovich— and I'd the sense he still loved her madly. I wondered if theirs was a tactical divorce, and so Acton's goin' to take a long look at her bank accounts and known-associates."

Williams tilted his head with interest. "Is Acton trying to bring-in Denisovich, on the Public Accounts case?"

"He hasn't exactly told me what his aim is, but he's actin' like a hound to the point about all this, and the ex-husband was the principal for the shell company that owned the burnt yachts. Not to mention that our Mr. Denisovich was jumpy as a tick when

Acton was askin' him questions, so I wouldn't be surprised if he knows somethin', even if he wasn't directly involved."

Williams suggested, "If he loves his ex-wife, maybe he's covering for her?"

But Doyle reminded him, "There's little point, since there's no one left to cover for anymore."

She looked out the window for a moment, thinking about this, and having the strong feeling that she was on the right track. "They divorced about three years ago—what was happenin', around then? Faith, so much is always goin' on that it's hard to remember, exactly. What happened, about three-or-so years ago, that would spook Denisovich into a tactical divorce?"

Thinking about it, Williams offered, "I don't think anyone had any suspicions about the Public Accounts case, as of three years ago. Howard's corruption case, maybe? That was in full swing."

"Mayhap," she said a bit doubtfully. "Although I don't think Acton knows why they split, and if it was because of the corruption case, you'd think he'd have guessed that."

He gave her an amused look. "It was around three years ago that Lizzie helped bust you out of Wexton Prison."

Doyle laughed. "Now, there's a memory—and not necessarily a fond one; although Edward was born, and he more than makes up for it." She knit her brow. "When did you marry Lizzie?"

"Much later, and it's hard to believe Sasha would seek a tactical divorce based on that particular news."

She held up her palms. "I'm just throwin' out ideas, Thomas. Think on it, please, because I've one of my feelings that if we figure out the reason for Sasha's divorce, we figure out how she fits into all this, and solve her murder."

He glanced at her. "No chance the ex-husband did it?"

"No," she said with conviction. "He'd have never hurt a hair on her head."

They turned into the Griffin Transport Company's parking lot, and he shifted the gear into park. "So; what's our goal today?"

"We're just nosin' around," she admitted. "I think there's a player who's slipped the net on Howard's murder—and so does Acton, by the way. The bureaucrats weren't smart enough to pull this off, and it certainly seems as though someone's bent on covering their tracks."

"And sending a message, considering the nature of Sasha's murder," he added. "Rival Russian mafia, maybe? They tend to be pretty ruthless."

"Mayhap; let's see what there is to see."

They entered the familiar industrial foyer at the Griffin Transport Company—the place that had figured prominently in the tainted-medication murders, being as one of their transport trucks was used, after-hours, to deliver the fateful medication batch to New View Pharmacy. Several of the company's employees had been duly arrested and charged with accessory-to-murder, despite their protestations that they'd known nothing about the plot. Nevertheless, their supervisor would testify that the personnel in question had specifically requested the after-hours run, and that they had then falsified their time-cards so as to obscure this fact. This circumstantial evidence had been enough to bind them over for trial, and a reasonable jury could easily find them guilty of conspiracy.

The receptionist was the same one they'd met once before, and she looked up to greet them with a little grimace. "Officers," she said. "I'm so glad we're finally going to turn a page from all this—it's been devastating for company morale. The brass are thinking about changing the company name, even though it's been the same for a hundred years."

"We're sorry for it," Williams sympathized. "But we appreciate the company's cooperation in helping to bring about justice."

She nodded. "If you'd like to speak to Ms. Piros about her trial testimony, she's in the back."

"That's more the job of the Crown Prosecutors," Williams explained. "We're here to ask a few follow-up questions of the other personnel, in case we missed something during the investigation."

Doyle asked, "Did anyone leave, ma'am, in the time period between the whistleblower's murder and the first time we came here, to speak with you?"

"Let me look," she said, and turned to her screen. "What were the dates, for both?"

Williams checked his tablet for this information, and the young woman then reviewed the personnel lists for the time period in question. "Here's one—Ahmed Tehrani. He failed to show up, and has never been back."

"Ahmed doesn't sound very Russian," Doyle joked to Williams.

The receptionist looked up. "We did hire Mr. Sergius, during that time period," she offered. "He's Russian."

And here I go, thought Doyle; headlong down another rabbit-hole.

CHAPTER 27

*T*entatively, Doyle asked, "Is Mr. Sergius—" here she paused, and then continued diplomatically, "Is he rather heavyset?"

"Somewhat," the receptionist acknowledged, in the same diplomatic tone.

Doyle turned to Williams. "He was a witness in the Health Professions Council case—well, not for the case itself, but for the retribution-murders that came after. He worked at Winchester University, back when I interviewed him."

Williams frowned slightly, because he'd already blown-up his morning schedule, courtesy of the fair Doyle, and he wasn't looking to sink any more time into this excursion. "Do you really think he might be significant?"

"Everythin' seems significant—it's that frustratin'," she admitted, and then she turned back to the receptionist. "I should say hallo to Mr. Sergius; is he workin' in the back?"

"Yes; he works in maintenance."

Williams, who was determined to stay on-track, added, "And we'll need to speak to Ahmed Tehrani's supervisor, also."

"Right—his supervisor was Ms. Piros."

Doyle and Williams exchanged a look; the reason Ahmed left so abruptly may have been because he'd become aware that his supervisor, Piros, was putting two-and-two together with respect to the accessories-to-murder. A very good reason to get out of town, if the man was a co-conspirator.

They thanked the receptionist, who buzzed them through the security door that led to the warehouse. Once inside, they paused for a moment, taking in the sight of the cavernous warehouse, which was echoing with the voices of busy people.

"Do you think Mr. Sergius is a suspect?" asked Williams. "We should have a strategy, if that's the case."

"I don't know what I'm thinkin'," Doyle admitted honestly. "He seemed a harmless sort of fellow when I met him, but on the other hand, it's a mighty big coincidence that we hear he's landed here at Griffin Transport, hard on my interview with a Russian kingpin this mornin'."

Williams nodded. "A suspect, then."

"I'd be surprised," Doyle admitted. "But you never know; as I recall, he did seem to have some knowledge of Russian mafia-types."

"Let's interview the supervisor, first," Williams decided. "And that way, Sergius will think he's not that important to us."

They approached Ahmed Tehrani's former supervisor, a tall, sturdy-looking woman who was overseeing the loading of strongboxes into a transport truck.

"Ms. Piros?" Williams asked, as he showed the woman his identification. "Do you have a moment?"

"For you, I do," she teased, and then signaled to a nearby man to come oversee the loading task. "How can I help you?"

. . .

Williams introduced them, and for a few minutes they discussed the upcoming murder trial, where the woman would be testifying about the co-conspirators she'd helped to catch.

Not nervous about it, a'tall, Doyle decided, sizing-up the witness. I think there's not a lot that would shake-up this one.

Williams offered, "We are following-up on a few loose-ends, and I note that an employee named Ahmed Tehrani left work immediately after the fentanyl deaths, but before a case had been opened by the police."

"That is correct," she agreed. "He didn't show up, one day— which wasn't much of a surprise. He didn't seem to like working here very much."

"Did he interact with the whistleblower—Enrique—during his time here?"

The woman gave Williams a knowing look, and offered, "Ahmed wasn't one to like Enrique, due to his sexual preferences." She winked. "So old-fashioned."

"Did you ever hear from Ahmed again?"

The supervisor shook her head. "No. He didn't even collect his wages owed."

Since any homicide detective worth his salt would find this last fact very interesting, Williams gave Doyle a glance.

Seeing the glance, the woman asked with a trace of amusement, "Why—do you think he's been murdered, too? I should quit—you wouldn't have any openings, would you?"

"Check with HR," Williams replied with a smile. "We're always looking for good coppers."

They thanked the supervisor, and then walked a small distance to an empty space where they could confer in private. Williams asked, "What do we have? It doesn't seem likely that Ahmed could be a suspect. This same supervisor was the one who grassed-out the others, and she'd have said something if she was suspicious."

But Doyle frowned. "I don't know—I'm inclined to think this Ahmed fellow was part of the scheme, Thomas. It would explain why he wasn't tryin' to make friends, and didn't want to work very hard. He knew it was only temporary."

But Williams tilted his head, skeptical. "This witness wouldn't have missed much. She seems very confident."

"Confident enough to be givin' you the green light," Doyle teased him.

With a small smile, he tilted his head. "I will neither confirm, nor deny."

She sighed. "You're a hazard, is what you are. And shame on her; you've a weddin' ring."

"You may be surprised to hear that the ring seems to act like catnip, for a lot of women."

"Then shame on them," she repeated, as they turned to walk toward the maintenance area. "And I'll say no more, since you've learned a hard lesson with Sasha. Here's hopin' this one doesn't turn up dead, too."

"I'm never going to live that down," Williams reflected aloud, to no one in particular.

But Doyle had already moved onto the next troubling topic. "You know, Thomas, that's two Persians, now, who've shown-up in this timeline only to disappear without a trace."

"Oh? Who's the other one?"

"Nazy's new beau, who—coincidentally enough—worked in Howard's building, at the security desk. I wonder if they're connected, somehow."

Williams shrugged, slightly. "I'm not sure that's significant, Kath."

"I suppose not," she agreed, since Williams didn't know about Sir Vikili's warning. She teetered on the edge of telling him, but decided she'd best not—best button her lip, lest she be called upon the carpet by Professional Standards for lack of ethnic sensitivity. Therefore, she concluded a bit lamely, "It just seems a bit odd."

As they made their way across the building's expansive concrete floor, he joked, "Poor Lizzie would like to disappear; Acton's having her lay the foundation at Howard's trial for all of the chain-of-custody evidence. There's a lot of it."

"Aye, I don't envy the poor lass. It doesn't help matters that all the direct evidence from Howard's flat has disappeared."

"Narcotics evidence does tend to disappear," he noted with a full measure of cynicism. "But in this case, it won't matter much because everyone already knows what happened—it was all over the press."

Doyle nodded, still a bit distracted as they approached the maintenance area. Williams wasn't inclined to chase any niggling loose ends, since the investigative process was finished and trial was looming. But Williams didn't have a ghost, prodding him about having missed something important—presumably, the true murderer.

And—come to think of it—wasn't it handy, that the direct evidence had disappeared and that the jury was already primed to convict? And wasn't it doubly-handy that Lizzie, Acton's henchman—or henchwoman, more correctly—was going to lay the foundation for the circumstantial evidence? If one were inclined to be a bit suspicious, one would almost have the impression that a certain Chief Inspector was steering this homicide trial exactly where he wanted it to go—which should be completely unnecessary; as Williams had pointed out, everyone already knew what had happened.

Made very uneasy by these troubling thoughts, Doyle decided that she'd test it out, to see how much Williams knew or didn't know. "Is it *possible*, Thomas, that there truly is another player out there? It would explain this sudden string of arson fires. And Denisovich was that nervous, which seemed unusual for the likes of him."

"There's always the possibility that someone got away," Williams acknowledged. "We have to go to trial with the evidence we have."

Tentatively she ventured, "Or mayhap the defendants, in this case, are bein' framed-up."

Surprised, he immediately cocked a skeptical brow. "That seems very unlikely, Kath—they've already held the preliminary hearing. You can't advance to trial unless the prosecutors have shown they have a decent case against these defendants."

"Unless the evidence has been cooked-up." She said it casually, but focused on his reaction like a laser beam.

But Williams seemed more puzzled by this remark, than anything else. "I'm just not seeing it, Kath. The evidence seems cut-and-dried."

It was the truth, which meant that Lizzie wasn't telling her husband about whatever mysterious project Acton was overseeing. Crossly, Doyle observed, "And even if it weren't cut-and-dried, Lizzie would never speak out-of-school—faith, Acton's minions are like a flippin' cult who are all stuck in the Middle Ages."

"She'd tell me," Williams insisted. "Especially if it was something that big."

Doyle nodded, thinking it best to keep her opinion to herself; after all, Williams was not as familiar with Trestles-folk as she was.

Already having a good guess as to what his answer would be,

she asked, "Should I take a quick look into our missin' Ahmed? Mayhap do a 'whereabouts' check?"

He shrugged, slightly. "I vote no, Kath. There's been no missing-persons report, after all—just a man who quit his job. I don't think we can justify it."

Doyle—who was forced to omit any and all pertinent ghost-warnings—nonetheless insisted, "I truly think someone's slipped the net, Thomas—someone important. Mayhap it's Ahmed."

But this suggestion didn't seem to faze him. "You have good instincts, Kath, and maybe you're right—someone's got away. But you know as well as I do, that a lot of people slip our net every day. I could name a dozen people, on the spot, who should rightfully be in prison."

This was unfortunately all too true. "Aye that," she reluctantly conceded. "All right—let's go follow-up on the Russian branch of this tangle. Faith, between the Russians and the Persians, I wonder if we're lookin' at some sort of turf-war?"

But he smiled slightly. "Not between the Russians and the Persians, Kath; they've been allies for centuries."

She stared at him in surprise. "Truly?"

"I'm beginning to think that history wasn't your strong suit."

"Nothin' truly was," she admitted, but she said it absently because this was important; the ghost had said something about this—about how his death was the result of ancient alliances, and ancient grudges. There's *something* to this tangle-patch, she thought; I'd bet my teeth—if only it all weren't so confusing.

Mr. Sergius was dressed in coveralls and wiping oil from his hands with a rag, as he spotted Doyle approaching. "Ha," the big man said, with an exaggerated grimace. "You, again."

"Me, again," Doyle smiled. "I'm that surprised to see you here, Mr. Sergius—how are you?"

"I am married, now," he replied, and waggled the finger that bore the ring. "And so, I cannot say that I am happy."

"I don't know if that's true," Doyle teased. "My congratulations."

He shrugged. "She is old-fashioned, and says, 'we must be married' and so I say 'ok'."

"A wise woman, to nail you down."

The big man unbent enough to smile. "She says I must exercise, and not sit at a desk all day. So, I take a different job."

"You do look healthier, Mr. Sergius."

"She gives me vitamins, and protein-powder." This, said in the scoffing tones of a man who is secretly well-pleased to be the object of such attention.

"How's our Bertie?—the dog," she explained, in an aside to Williams.

The man made a deprecatory gesture with his hands. "Fah—he is old, and fat. We take him to the dog park every day—more exercise for me," he groused, but again, Doyle knew that he was secretly well-pleased.

"D'you like this work? It's so different, from your last."

He shrugged. "I like the machines. And I will try-out to be a driver, soon; the money is good. My cousin, he got me the job, here." He lowered his voice, and said to Doyle with some significance, "He knows people."

Dredging up the memory, Doyle remembered the term the man had once used to refer to a mafia-boss. "Your cousin knows a *pakhan*?"

"No, no," he chuckled. "My cousin knows the Frenchman. That is much better than a *pakhan*."

"Ah," said Doyle in a knowing manner, as she touched Williams' arm in warning. "Say no more."

CHAPTER 28

"$\mathcal{M}$other a' Mercy, but I've *truly* got to start writin' everythin' down," Doyle complained, as she climbed into Williams' car. "There's too far much for my poor brain to remember." She remembered to add, "Hence."

"Was he referring to Savoie?"

"Aye, I think so." Doyle decided she'd best say no more, because—lest we forget—Acton and Savoie had originally set-up the Public Accounts skimming rig, and so the reference to Savoie's involvement, in the transport company was not wholly unexpected. She wasn't certain whether Williams was aware of this troubling little fact, however, and so she should probably err on the side of caution, and button her lip.

But Williams didn't seem to be overly-concerned about Savoie's name suddenly popping up. "I don't think it means anything, Kath—it's not even surprising. We know that Savoie came to England to take over Solonik's rigs, and Solonik was Russian. It only stands to reason—if Savoie's their guv, now—that he's got some pull within the Russian mafia-community."

Doyle made a skeptical sound. "Why would the Russians do what a Frenchman tells them to?"

"Money," he said succinctly. "And these underworld-types always want a strong horse in charge; if Savoie took-out Solonik, he fills that bill."

"I suppose," she agreed.

He smiled, slightly. "So; now France has entered the game, along with Russia and Persia."

"Aye—it's like a criminal League of Nations around here." Doyle mused. "Ancient alliances and ancient grudges."

He glanced at her in surprise. "I can see the alliances, but who's got a grudge?"

"Acton," she replied thoughtfully. "Acton's got a mighty grudge."

Alarmed, he half-joked, "Not against me, I hope?"

"No—you're my friend, so you've got immunity. Not to mention you fished me out of the Thames, once upon a time."

Her scalp prickled, and she paused in surprise. No question, that Williams had come to her rescue, and therefore Acton would always protect him come what may; but why was that important?

"It was a pleasure," Williams joked. "Although the water was pretty cold."

But she continued distracted, with the feeling that—whatever was going on, here—she was tantalizingly close to finding out what the ghost was getting at.

Aloud, she mused, "I feel as though I keep pullin' at threads, but I haven't pulled the right one, as yet—the one that unravels it all."

He cocked his head toward her. "Not sure what we're talking about."

"Neither am I," she admitted.

"So; are we doing a report?" Williams added, a bit pointedly.

She quirked her mouth. "By which you mean, is your DS doin' a report?"

"It's your call," he offered. "Like I said, it doesn't seem worth the time, since the trial's already spooled-up. I don't think we've uncovered anything earth-shaking—and even if we found any new evidence, it would have to be shared with the defense, who'd immediately ask for a postponement. I just don't think it's worth the follow-up."

"No—you're right." He made a good point; in the interest of fairness, the prosecution always had to share whatever evidence they'd collected with the defense, and share it well ahead of time so that the defense could prepare to counter it. In this case, the trial was indeed all spooled-up, and looked to be a foregone conclusion. If only the fair Doyle didn't have the feeling that she should be un-spooling it, as fast as she was able.

They approached the car, and he asked, "Are we going back to headquarters?"

"No—I've got to get home to Tommy with all speed, if you wouldn't mind droppin' me there." She added sincerely, "Thanks so much for indulgin' me, DI Williams, even though I squeaked on you about Sasha."

"Lesson learned," he repeated philosophically, and started the car.

CHAPTER 29

$\mathcal{D}$oyle grimaced as she hurried down the hallway toward her flat. She could hear Tommy squalling, even through the walls.

"I'm that sorry," she said to Reynolds, as she lifted the unhappy baby from his bouncing arms. "It took longer than I thought."

"Not at all, madam," said the butler, over the din.

With no further ado, she sank into the sofa and put the baby to breast, wincing, because it was a bit painful, with her breasts so full.

"I did attempt to give him a bottle, madam, but he was not interested."

"Mum!" Edward called out from the stairs, as he emerged to run toward her. "Miss Callie won't go to the park."

"We'll all go, after lunch," Doyle soothed.

But the older boy was unhappy, and clung to her neck, crowding the baby. "Put Tommy down."

"Come along, Edward," Callie offered, as the girl held out a hand to her wayward charge. "Give your mum some space."

"That's all right, Callie," Doyle smiled; "I used to pray I'd have a family, some day, and here I am in spades." She drew Edward close, and asked, "Tell me what you did this mornin'; I've missed you to flinders."

Somewhat mollified, the little boy began to relate the morning's activities whilst the other adults quietly retreated to set-up the lunch-table.

During lunch, Doyle asked Callie about her family, since she hadn't touched base with her recently. "How's your mum and da?"

"They're great—although they're not very happy about the investigation."

Doyle gave the girl a sympathetic look, because it was indeed a miserable mess; Callie's birth-mother, Melinda, was trying to entice the girl into moving-in with her, and Callie's adoptive parents—nice people, from the village near Acton's estate—were understandably dismayed by this intrusion into their happy and routine lives. And—in addition to that rough adjustment—they'd been forced to contend with the private investigators who were looking into Melinda's husband's death.

Melinda had secretly married an RC priest—of all things, and shame on her—and then the poor man had died almost immediately after. Since he'd a fortune in a family trust, Melinda was suddenly wealthy, with the dead priest's mother very unhappy about this turn of events and suspicioning that Melinda had done him in. Since the mother—Lady Madeline—was minor aristocracy with a fortune at her back, she was sparing no expense in her attempt to go after Melinda.

And good luck to her, thought Doyle; as it turned out, Callie was Acton's half-sister—they'd shared the same questionable father—and so, Lady Madeline and her paltry investigators had little chance of success, even if they weren't yet aware of this pertinent little fact. The same mantle of immunity that had been thrown over Doyle's friends would be thrown over Callie and Melinda, and that mantle was a mighty one.

But, in the meantime, the situation was thoroughly uncomfortable for everyone involved. In fact, Doyle was rather surprised that Acton hadn't moved to resolve the matter already, either by rattling his formidable sword, or by shoveling money toward the bereft mother. After all, the woman had every right to be upset; her only son had died under questionable circumstances —not to mention he'd done a shameful thing, with the secret marriage—and so, she was somewhat of a figure of sympathy.

With a little smile, Doyle asked the girl, "Is our Melinda mindin' herself?"

"She's improving," Callie explained with an answering smile. "I've had to be firm about setting boundaries, and I think it's helped."

"Good one," said Doyle, and was secretly much relieved. Poor Callie had been knocked off her pins by all these events, and so she'd been behaving a bit badly. Small blame to her, of course, but Doyle now had the sense that the girl had found her feet, and was much more herself, again.

"Is she movin'?" Doyle asked. "Are you?" Now that she could afford it, Melinda wanted to move into a gated property in the suburbs, and was trying to convince Callie to move-in with her. It was a bit uncomfortable, truly, because Melinda was on a mission to make-up for lost time, and was therefore smothering poor Callie with money and affection.

As she helped Edward wipe his hands, Callie replied, "We've come to a compromise of sorts. She's going to move into a flat here in London, and I'll have a flat close by."

"That's a fine idea," Doyle agreed. "You'll want to have your own space, and be able to come and go without havin' to check in. Which neighborhood?"

"A few streets from here, as a matter of fact. The real estate representative showed me around, yesterday." She paused to confide, "He was very persuasive."

"Meanin' he was handsome, which seems to be the most important qualification, for real estate representatives," Doyle noted. "Faith, but it'll be grand, to have you within walkin' distance Callie."

"Yes. I'm trying to decide whether to go back to school—perhaps become a teacher."

"Acton will be happy to pay for it," Doyle volunteered. "If you don't want to be overly-dependent on Melinda."

"Thank you—I'm still sorting it out." She paused, and then ventured, "Have you heard from Miss Valerie? I can help out as much as you'd like."

This was rather unexpected, and put Doyle in a cleft stick, because she'd the strong feeling Acton was still a bit cross with his half-sister, and wouldn't necessarily want her underfoot—at least for a while. On the other hand, having the girl underfoot might go a long ways toward calming those troubled waters—Acton should see that Callie was making the effort to right herself, and—after all —she was family.

After deciding that a compromise was in order, Doyle assured her, "That's very kind of you, Callie—let me consult with Acton; I imagine we'll hire a new full-time nanny, if we find out for certain that Miss Valerie's done a bunk, but you can always assist."

Callie expressed her gratitude, and Doyle wondered if perhaps the girl was also looking for an independent means of income, which wasn't a bad idea, given the Melinda-situation.

But she was suddenly reminded of another possible

motivation, when Callie ventured a bit self-consciously, "How is Emile? Do you still see him at the park, every day?"

Oh-oh, Doyle thought; that's right—poor Callie had carried a mighty torch for Philippe Savoie, and it was fortunate that the Frenchman had never encouraged her in the slightest—speaking of things that would make Acton cross. Doubly-cross, since he was unhappy with the both of them, just now.

Casually, Doyle replied, "Faith, I haven't seen the boyo in a good while—first, I had our Tommy, and then, we were on holiday."

"Oh—oh, of course." The girl lowered her head to listen to Edward, who'd decided that the grown-ups were talking to each other altogether too much, and should pay a bit more attention to him.

Poor Callie, thought Doyle, as she returned to her meal; she's young and pretty, but doomed to discover that she's been beaten-out by a twice-widowed mother of two. She's rather like Gabriel, in being star-crossed, and longing after the wrong person—it's that atom-bomb thing, again. A shame, that we can't control the uncontrollable; instead, we can only hope that everything happens for a reason, but I suppose that's little comfort when dealing with unrequited love—I'd be settling into the Yorkshire Dales myself, faster than the twitch of a cat's tail.

CHAPTER 30

*A*fter lunch, Doyle was happy to go on a park-excursion, mainly because she was in dire need of a walkabout so as clear her mind, and think over the various things she'd learned today. Often when she mulled things over, something would stand out as important—something that she'd missed, earlier.

Although there'd be little chance for solitude, unfortunately—taking a walk over to the park nowadays necessarily involved an entourage; aside from Callie, Doyle would also be accompanied by Reynolds and Trenton, being as Doyle's husband was a cautious man when it came to his family.

Originally, Doyle had chafed at this inconvenience but she'd grown accustomed; not only was Acton wealthy and famous, but he'd made some powerful enemies, along the way, and it paid to be vigilant—they'd weathered a few disturbing events where Edward had been put at risk, and so Doyle was more than willing to tolerate the lack of spontaneity in their lives.

The usual afternoon visitors were already at the playground, and Doyle smiled a greeting at Mary, sitting on a bench beside baby Hannah's pram whilst Gemma played on the monkey-bars.

And—speak of the devil—Philippe Savoie was also present, along with his son, Emile. Savoie usually brought Emile to the playground after school, as it was within walking distance, and that little boyo was one who would need to expend some pent-up energy after sitting in a classroom all day.

At present, Savoie stood at the playground's perimeter and keeping an eye on his son, who was currently involved in a noisy contest with some other boys to see who could jump the furthest from a line in the sand.

Edward, of course, did not hesitate to run over to join them as fast as his little legs could carry him.

"You can't play," one of the other boys pronounced with impatience. "You're too little."

"He can too play," Emile decided. "He can jump against himself, is all."

"May I play?" Gemma asked, a bit shyly.

"No, you're a girl."

"I bet she can jump further than you," Emile countered.

"No, she can't," the other boy disagreed hotly, and the matter was immediately put to the test, with the result that—whilst Gemma could not jump as far as the older boy—she'd proved her mettle, and was allowed to participate.

Doyle stood watching them for a few moments, gently jiggling the chest-carrier and hoping that Tommy would please, please settle into sleep—he'd been thrown off, by having a late feeding, and now he was a bit fussy.

Whilst she waited for the baby to succumb to the jiggling, she duly noted that Callie had gone over to greet Mary, carefully not looking at Savoie, and that Mary was also carefully not looking at

Savoie, despite the fact there was a humming resonance stretching between the two.

So; there's been more raging-sex, goin' on, thought Doyle—and I shouldn't be surprised in the least; it's not an easy thing to give up, once you've had a taste. Father John's going to have to put-up a swinging door in the confessional—not that he didn't predict this whole turn of events, of course, which just goes to show that I haven't been paying attention, lately. Neither has Acton, for that matter.

She paused, wondering where this errant little thought had come from. Acton was a payer-of-attention like no other, but it did seem as though all his brooding and fretting had been eating-up his paying-attention time, and he'd missed something—something important. He'd missed it, in the same way that he'd missed how Nazy's beau was a dodgy character, and how people seemed to be disappearing, including the aforementioned dodgy character.

And—come to think of it—it sounded as though Ahmed—who'd disappeared from the transport company—was something of a dodgy character, also. She wondered, for a moment, if he'd disappeared before or after Mr. Sergius had been hired.

With a mental shake, she scolded herself for diving headfirst down yet another rabbit hole; she'd the sure sense that Mr. Sergius was exactly what he seemed—a rather overweight, brash Russian man in the best tradition, who was miles more interested in where his next pint was coming from than in any paltry murder investigation. He'd been very unconcerned about the last one, after all, and now she understood why this was: he knew people.

Slowly, she lifted her gaze to stare into the distance. Mr. Sergius knew people—or at least, he had relatives who knew people—which meant that he shouldn't be left out of the growing slate of Russian characters who seemed to feature largely in this tale. Mayhap this Russian thread was the one that she needed to pull.

Because she'd gone still, Tommy started fretting again, and so she re-instituted the jiggling-protocol as she pulled her mobile. After raising the transport company's receptionist, she asked, "If you don't mind, I wanted to check on a couple of dates for my report; I'll need to know when Mr. Tehrani quit, as well as the date that Mr. Sergius was hired."

The woman gave the information, and Doyle thanked her before ringing off. So; Tehrani had disappeared a week after Sergius had started—there was a one-week overlap, between the two employees. Hard to believe, that Sergius had anything to do with anything, but people were dropping from sight, and—despite his appearance—Doyle knew that the man was not stupid; after all, he was the one who'd twigged the true purpose of the Winchester University night-class. He'd twigged them, because he knew how mafia-types operated—not to mention that he hadn't turned a hair when dodgy characters had started disappearing in that case.

Suddenly brought up short, Doyle realized there was a huge flaw in her dodgy-characters-are-disappearing theory, because it seemed very unlikely that the bookkeeper at church was dodgy, and she was one of the disappearees—if there was such a word—in this tangle.

Fortunately, Doyle had a ready witness at hand to test it out, and so—with a casual air—she strolled over to where Mary was seated on the bench, minding baby Hannah and carefully ignoring Savoie.

Callie had gone over to supervise Edward, and so the two young mothers greeted one another in quiet tones, so as to let sleeping babies lie.

Doyle began, "I'm meetin'-up with Nellie, later today; she's that worried because the church bookkeeper hasn't shown-up for a few days, and Nellie doesn't think she's the type to shirk."

"Oh—no," breathed Mary with all concern. "I hope Mrs. Rossa's all right; I don't think she has any family in the area— she's an immigrant, from Eastern Europe."

Doyle stared at her, and decided that this was one coincidence too far, even for someone already as rabbit-holed as she was. Therefore, she ventured, "D'you think she's the type to get into trouble—a bit dodgy, mayhap?"

"Oh—oh, not at all." Mary shook her head with some certainty. "She's a very nice woman—quiet, but very nice." With a worried frown, she repeated, "I hope she's all right."

"I'm sure it's nothin'," Doyle lied, and considered the fact that her dodgy-characters theory did seem to be flawed—although Mary probably wouldn't recognize a dodgy-character if she saw one, with Savoie serving as an excellent case-in-point. Mary always saw the good in everyone—*her ways are the ways of gentleness, and all her paths are peace*, the ghost had said.

Which was important, of course; Doyle was fast-coming to the realization that every word the ghost had said was somehow important. Mary was wonderfully kind but rather naïve, and Doyle had been tasked with saving her—although what she was supposed to be saving her from was unclear. She'd presumed the ghost wanted to save her from Savoie, but mayhap it was something having to do with these disappearing people, and her late husband's murder trial.

With a mighty effort, Doyle steered away from yet another distraction and brought herself back to the subject at hand. "Did Mrs. Rossa ever tell you anythin' that might be helpful, in trackin' her down? Did she ever talk about returnin' to her home country, for instance?"

Frowning, Mary considered this. "No—she seemed very

happy, here. I think she was a homebody and didn't go out much. She did love the theatre, though."

Again, this seemed a coincidence too far and Doyle ventured, "Was she a Sasha Lanska fan?"

"I'm not sure who that is," Mary confessed.

"She was a Russian actress is all, so I just wondered. Did you know if Mrs. Rossa belonged to a group called the Mossovet?"

Slowly, Mary shook her head. "I never heard mention. She did attend the Russian Orthodox Church, here in town."

Doyle blinked. "She didn't attend St. Michael's?"

"No—she was ROC, and not RC," the young woman explained, "I only know, because Mrs. Mackey attended their service when she was visiting, and she asked after Mrs. Rossa—I think she was surprised that she hadn't seen her at church."

This seemed rather ominous, and Doyle persisted, "Did Mrs. Rossa have any hobbies or interests that she spoke of?"

"She was a baker," Mary offered. "Nellie told her that I baked, and so we exchanged recipes—it's always interesting when you can try-out new things, from a different culture."

Doyle decided that she may as well ask—she was deep, deep down this particular rabbit-hole, anyway. "Did you give her your recipe for bread-puddin'?"

Mary smiled. "There was no need; they have something very similar in their tradition—*pirog*, I think she called it."

So much for that rabbit-hole. Nevertheless, Doyle decided that she may as well add, "Nigel loved your bread-puddin', I think."

But Mary only shook her head. "No, Lady Acton—it's my Gemma, who loves bread-pudding. Nigel never liked it—he never liked anything that was too heavy."

"Oh," said Doyle, who stared at her, unsure of what to say.

With a small smile, Mary explained, "I use a muffin-tin, and on Sundays I bake Gemma five little bread-puddings, so that she may bring them to school for her dessert." A bit guiltily, she added, "She loves it so, and she's so slim; I don't think there's any harm in it."

"No, indeed," Doyle agreed, who was fast-coming to the conclusion that this particular rabbit-hole was a dead end, and let this be a lesson.

"I hope Mrs. Rossa is all right," Mary repeated, worried. "It does seem unlike her, to simply not show up."

Doyle made a wry mouth. "Well, gird your loins, Mary; our wretched nanny isn't showin' up, either, and I'll soon be needin' another, if you don't mind."

"Oh—" said Mary, as her cheeks turned pink. "Oh—"

The young woman paused, a bit flustered, and Doyle managed to avoid glancing in Savoie's direction as she quickly put two-and-two together. Instead, with a casual air, she soothed, "No worries, Mary; if you've reconsidered, I completely understand. I just thought to give you the right of first refusal before we go back to the agency again."

Mary lowered her voice, as she confided, "I'm not supposed to say, Lady Acton, but I don't want you to think I'm being ungrateful. Philippe is investing in a bakery, and he's asked if I wouldn't mind managing it."

CHAPTER 31

*D*oyle blinked. "Is he, indeed?"

Mary nodded, her eyes alight. "Philippe wanted to make it into a French bakery, but I didn't think we should limit it only to French goods—I'd like to use my recipes, and Lizzie's, too."

"Well, that sounds wonderful, Mary, and just what you'd like. Say goodbye to your nannyin' days."

The other woman offered, "It won't happen right away, Lady Acton—Philippe said some renovations will be needed, first. I'd be happy to help in the meantime."

"We'll see—I may be ahead of myself, anyways. Mayhap the wretched Miss Valerie will make a reappearance, with some ready explanation for goin' doggo."

"Have you checked with her church?"

Doyle frowned, as she was fairly certain Miss Valerie had never spoken of attending a church. "Which church is this, Mary?"

"I think she attends the same church as Mrs. Rossa—the ROC one."

It's a rare wonder, thought Doyle as she stared at the other woman, that I've not run barkin' mad—although mayhap I have, and I'm one of those people who doesn't realize it, like the kooks who wander into the Yard and sincerely tell the police that the space aliens are after them. And—speaking of people who are half-mad—I wonder if Acton knows about this; after all, he hasn't been paying attention lately.

Tommy began to stir again, and so Doyle whispered, "I've got to walk, Mary," and the other young mother nodded in understanding.

As she began to slowly circle the playground—bouncing a bit, for emphasis—Doyle made a mental note to ask Acton about this church-wrinkle. Again, it seemed more than a coincidence, that two women who'd come into their orbit, lately, were attending the same ROC church and then had disappeared—although mayhap it didn't mean anything, and she was getting as paranoid as her half-mad husband. Hopefully, Mrs. Mackey wasn't slated to disappear also.

I'll speak with Acton, she decided—as soon as Tommy settles himself down, poor boyo.

Keeping up her bouncing pace, it dawned on Doyle that Mary hadn't once mentioned the upcoming murder trial—which she'd been dreading just a short time ago—and decided that Savoie must be using this bakery-project to distract the young widow—and good on him, if that was his intent. Strange, that the fair Doyle was supposed to save Mary; between the raging-sex and the bakery-project it didn't seem as though she was in much need of saving. Unless Doyle was supposed to save her from those very things, of course—this particular ghost was not someone who'd show up for no reason, and it was past time she stopped being such a baby and had a few words with our Mr. Savoie.

Therefore, she mentally girded her loins as she made a turn 'round the perimeter of the fence, but was suddenly brought up short. There was a dog, sitting at a small distance with his back against the fence, and watching the children play. But he was not just any dog.

Holy Mother, thought Doyle in abject surprise, as she belatedly remembered to keep jiggling the baby-carrier.

The dog was a large one—a fierce-looking, no-nonsense kind of dog; but he had one truly outstanding characteristic, which was that he was no longer alive.

A ghost-dog, thought Doyle, as she regarded him in astonishment. Now, here's a crackin' wrinkle.

And—despite the fact she was surely the only one present who knew of his existence—the dog was roundly ignoring her. Which was to the good, she supposed, since dogs—live ones, at least—tended to bark at her and make an embarrassing fuss.

Best leave him be, she decided, as she recalled herself to her errand; he doesn't look to be causing any trouble—mayhap he has fond memories of this park. Strange, that I've never seen another, though.

Pinning on a determined smile, she headed over toward Savoie, who turned his head to watch her approach with an impassive expression. Only Doyle realized that he wasn't feeling impassive—not at all.

With some surprise, she halted before him. "Are you angry with me, Philippe?"

"*Non-non,*" he assured her immediately, but it was not exactly the truth.

Mother a' Mercy, but he's angry, she realized. Another wrathful man; but why? She then recalled that the last time they'd had a little heart-to-heart, she'd scolded him—mayhap that was it; he was not one who liked to be scolded. And this, of course, did not bode well, since the fair Doyle was planning to quiz him about his Mary-intentions, which were truly none of her business save that a ghost was making it her business.

Therefore, she thought she'd start out, "I don't think you've met baby Tommy as yet."

She bent her knees a bit, so that he could peer within the carrier.

Softening, he observed with a small smile, *"Le bon bébé. Bien."*

With a show of heartiness, Doyle continued, "He'll be out there with Emile and Edward before you know it. We'll be outnumbered."

His gaze slid to meet hers. "And Gemma, *aussi.*"

"Aye," she readily agreed. "Gemma's holdin' her own with the others. I think Emile's been a good influence; remember when she wouldn't say boo to a goose?"

He cocked his head.

"It means that she was very shy, and didn't like to speak up."

He nodded, thoughtfully. *"Bien.* I tell the gooses, now."

She smiled in acknowledgement; he'd definitely stepped-in to help Mary's family, and since this seemed to be a good opening she decided she'd best take it—wrathful or no. "Don't think I can't see how you're helpin' to take care of our Mary, Philippe—and I'm sure it's much-appreciated."

In response, he only tilted his head in acknowledgement—not one to kiss and tell, was Philippe Savoie. It was a shame, truly; he tended to hold his cards very close to the vest—just as Acton did —and it would have been miles easier if he'd give her more of an opening.

With some determination, she ventured, "Mary's very fond of you, I think."

He was amused, suddenly—she could sense it, even though his impassive expression did not change. He knows exactly what I'm doing, here, she thought, as she felt her color rise.

"Sorry," she readily confessed. "I suppose I'm worried about—about the situation."

"The situation, it is well," he pronounced.

Thoroughly embarrassed, Doyle felt she should at least make a push, however unwelcome. Therefore, in a constrained tone she added, "Mary's had a rough go, lately."

"*Oui*," he agreed, and offered nothing more.

At a loss, she bid him goodbye and took her leave, turning so as to make another circuit around the playground. Tommy seemed disinclined to sleep, and so she should take him out of the carrier soon, and mayhap feed him again.

As she walked away, she noted that the rather large man who'd been standing within the gate shifted his position, because she'd obstructed his view of the playground. With a small smile of greeting, Doyle walked past the man, and duly noted that Trenton had shifted his own position so as keep eyes on their interaction.

Savoie's brought security, Doyle concluded, and Trenton's like a bird on a wire about it. And—now that she'd a good look at the man—she wouldn't be at all surprised if Savoie's security-man was Mr. Sergius' cousin; they'd the same look, although this man was taller and in far better shape.

It was rather surprising, actually; she was almost certain Savoie had never brought security with him before—after all, who'd take-on Savoie? Even Denisovich was afraid of him.

Oh, she suddenly realized, and made a mighty effort not to turn and stare at the security-man. Oh; I know exactly who would take-on Savoie.

Thoroughly dismayed, she jostled Tomm, and tried to tamp

down an acute sense of alarm, even as she scolded herself for leaping to ridiculous conclusions. Come now, lass, it was silly to think that Acton was gunning for Savoie—wasn't it? Save that such a turn of events would certainly fit the facts on the ground; for the first time ever, Savoie didn't wish to speak with her—wary, he was. And meanwhile, Acton was a'boil, and eaten-up with rage—which was very unlike him, actually. Acton was a quiet plotter, rather than a rager. He was the fox, in that gingerbread-man story—all guileful and polite 'till it was too late, and you were all eaten-up.

But Acton wasn't being very guileful and polite, just now—he was that angry, and—for that matter—so was Savoie. Mayhap, then, it wasn't the gingerbread-man story a'tall; mayhap it was that other one—that Hector-and-Achilles story. The two stories were quite different, despite what Reynolds had said; there was no polite guilefulness, in the Greek one—instead everyone raged about until they all wound up dead.

Her scalp started prickling like a live thing and she closed her eyes, briefly, trying to remember what Reynolds had told her. Achilles had sworn revenge because Hector had killed a friend. And Achilles had prevailed, in their big showdown, because he'd known where Hector's weakness was. But then—in true Greek fashion—everyone was caught-up in a burning ball of pride that laid waste to everyone, winners and losers alike.

With a sudden burst of clarity, her eyes flew open. Of course—faith, but she was a knocker not to have realized it before now—after all, there was a dead friend who featured prominently in the current tale, and that dead friend's ghost had been staring her in the face and politely asking for vengeance. He was asking for vengeance, because a player had slipped the net, and Acton must be convinced that Savoie was the one who'd done the slipping. Holy Mother of God—Acton thought Savoie killed Howard;

Savoie, who was moving himself into the dead man's place with Mary as slick as an otter.

And small wonder that Acton didn't want her to know what was eating him up and causing him to walk, a'nights. Acton was furious, and determined to be the Achilles in this tale—hell-bent on meting out a full measure of vengeance.

Save for the troubling fact that he was wrong. After all, if Acton was busy avenging Nigel Howard's death, then the man wouldn't be haunting the fair Doyle's dreams and pushing her to do a bit of vengeance-seeking, herself. Acton was the grand master in the vengeance-seeking business, and he'd not need an assist from the likes of the fair Doyle.

But an assist was apparently needful, because the very friend who'd been killed was now haunting her—haunting her, and warning her that wrath tends to cloud your judgment, whilst all the while Acton was a boiling cauldron of wrath.

"Saints and *holy* angels," she said aloud. "Sorry, Tommy—your mum's got a Code One."

She promptly pulled her mobile and rang-up Acton on their private line.

"Kathleen," he answered quietly. He must be in a meeting, then. "May I call you back?"

"No," she replied. "You've got to drop whatever you're doin', husband, and come meet me."

There was a small pause. "What is this about?"

She made a face, because behind his polite tone he was wary, and hadn't even asked if she was all right, which just went to show how well he could read her voice. "I'm not goin' to say over the phone—it's a face-to-face thing. One of those non-discussions that you and I are so very good at."

There was another small pause. "How much trouble am I in?"

"Nothin' that can't be mended, husband. But—as usual—

you're goin' about thinkin' that you're bulletproof, but if you're not careful you're goin' to wind up like *Cú Chulainn*."

There was yet another small pause. "And who is that?"

"Someone who let his ego get in the way of his good sense," she informed him. "The stupid Greeks aren't the only ones who can tell an epic tale."

CHAPTER 32

*B*ack at the playground, Doyle explained to Reynolds that she was slated to meet-up with Acton for a walk, over by the west gate, and that—if he and Callie would bring Edward home with them—she'd see them later back at the flat.

The servant raised his brows. "Very good, madam; make certain to bring Mr. Trenton along with you."

"Not bringin' Trenton," she advised; "I'd rather he stayed with you and Edward. Don't worry; if anyone gives me any guff, I will shoot them dead."

Reynolds, who didn't always approve of Doyle's sense of humor, said only, "As you say, madam."

Doyle then headed over to the west gate, trying to decide how to broach this latest sensitive topic with her husband, and then deciding that she wasn't much of a planner, so there was little point to it. First things first, anyways; Tommy was due for a nappy-change, and so she found a likely bench, and hauled the wee lad out of his chest carrier.

"Sorry," she said to her son, as he lay on his back, surprised, and squinting against the sunlight. "My other job keeps creepin' into this one."

Tommy cooed with delight at being thus addressed, and Doyle had to smile, because Tommy always seemed to think that everything was a big lark. A shame, that he'd have to grow up and temper his expectations. Babies are good for us, she decided, as she snapped-up his playsuit; they tend to remind us not to over-think things.

And hard on this thought, Doyle was hailed by her husband, who approached from the gate. Upon sighting his father, Tommy wriggled with wheezing delight, and so Acton lifted him from Doyle even as he leaned to kiss her. "Is everything all right?"

"No, it's not," she replied. "Holy Mother, Michael; you think Savoie killed Nigel Howard."

He was silent for a moment, as he settled the baby against his shoulder. Buying time, he was, to decide how best to fashion an answer—no easy thing, with the man's wife being how she was.

Finally, he offered, "It is possible."

Frowning, she considered this as she they fell into step together. "I don't see it."

Acton cast her a look. "He is certainly capable."

But slowly, she shook her head. "No."

"You are friends, and it may color your perception."

"You may know a lot about a lot of things," she replied. "But it's me, who knows people."

"Not always," he reminded her gently.

This was, of course, an excellent point, and she'd the bullet wounds to show for it. "All right, then—let's hear your case; why d'you think he did it?"

"He was involved in the fentanyl rig, at Wexton Prison."

She nodded in acknowledgement. "A good point—and I gave him a bear-garden jawin' about it, which I think took root, Michael

—I honestly do. Not to mention Savoie's a wily one, and unlikely to choose a mode for murder that would point such a shiny-bright arrow right back at him."

"That is a fair point, but I am afraid there is more."

Oh-oh, thought Doyle; here's something.

Her husband regarded the trees that branched overhead for a moment. "He killed Lady Abby, so as to try and frame Howard for her death."

She stared at him, agog. "Holy *Mother*, Michael."

"Indeed."

Slowly, Doyle reasoned, "Because he wanted Mary for himself."

"Yes. Because he wanted Mary for himself."

Doyle walked a few paces, thinking this over whilst Tommy made happy-baby noises, and clutched his fists into the fancy fabric of his father's suit.

With a small frown, Doyle offered, "I don't know as that's a clincher, Michael; again, the mode doesn't quite fit. If he truly wanted Howard out of the way, he would have just killed the man and have done. He's not as complicated as you are; he's miles more direct."

Her scalp started prickling, and she wondered why this was; Savoie wasn't nearly as guileful as Acton—instead, Savoie was all sharp-elbows and controlled menace. Surely, that went without saying?

"I'm afraid the evidence is irrefutable, with respect to Lady Abby."

But Doyle only said, "Oh—I believe you, and I don't doubt that he wanted her dead—Lady Abby kept threatenin' Mary, remember? She was a crackin' crazy-bird, with a tendency toward violence. So, Savoie decided to do her in, with the added benefit that her death would expose Howard as having fathered a child that he was neglectin'." Doyle glanced up at her husband. "Savoie knew Mary wouldn't have liked that, much, and—after all—he didn't know that it wasn't Howard's child in the first place. None of us did."

Almost apologetically, her husband tilted his head toward hers. "You may be clutching at straws, I'm afraid."

She blew out a breath. "I know—I sound like the mums who defend their sons, after they've landed in Detention. But I'm serious, Michael—my hand on my heart—even though it's hard for me to explain."

With a knit brow, she made an effort to put her instinct into words. "Savoie's got a kind of—a kind of *code*, I'd suppose you'd say. He killed Lady Abby because she kept threatenin' Mary, and —as an added bonus—he could implicate Howard, and expose the fact that he'd been unfaithful and was a deadbeat father— which he sincerely believed, until we all found out that such was not the case. But—even thinkin' the worst—he's not goin' to outright murder Mary's husband; he wouldn't do that to her. And he's not goin' to kill a bunch of innocent people in the process— that's just not who he is."

She could sense that her husband wasn't convinced, and so she added, "At heart, Savoie's a rescuer, Michael—strange as that may seem. Only look at me, and Martina Betancourt, and Emile. Faith, even Blakney said that Savoie was a fair gov, after Savoie took over Solonik's rigs."

"Bill Blakney?" Acton was understandably confused as to why Doyle would be referencing a minor witness from an old case.

Hastily, she moved on. "And besides, if Savoie truly killed Howard, he wouldn't leave the body lyin' about for the coppers to trace back to him. He's too seasoned for that; the body wouldn't be found unless he wanted it to be found—just like with Lady Abby."

Suddenly, she came to an abrupt halt, her eyes wide. "Holy *Mother*, Michael; could Savoie be the one who's killed Sasha Lanska?"

Acton regarded her in surprise, as he shifted Tommy to his other shoulder. "Why would Savoie kill Sasha Lanska?"

Slowly, she shook her head. "I don't know. I only thought of it because her burnt corpse is on full display, and he's that furious. Faith, it would explain why everyone's scatterin' like geese."

In a reasonable tone, Acton pointed out, "I sincerely doubt that Savoie would take-on the Russian mafia, Kathleen. He would be working with them, instead of against them. He took over Solonik's rigs, and there hasn't been any indication that there are ill feelings."

This, of course, was a very good point—unlikely, that Savoie would turn around and go scorched-earth on his business cohorts. Nonetheless, Doyle insisted, "I think he may have killed her. He's killed Sasha, but he didn't kill Howard."

"I don't know how you can be so certain."

"I don't know *either*, Michael," she said crossly. "For heaven's sake."

He was immediately contrite. "I beg your pardon," he soothed. "It's a bit chilly; allow me to give you my jacket."

"Only because Tommy's thoroughly ruined it," she said, continuing to be cross with him.

He paused to hand her the baby, and then drape his jacket around her shoulders. In the process, he leaned to look into her eyes. "I will look into your suggestions; I shouldn't doubt you— forgive me."

Mollified, she replied, "Recall that I've saved the day, and many a time."

"Indeed," he agreed. "It is only that it seems so unlikely."

With some exasperation, she observed, "It only seems unlikely because you're all bound up in bein' wrathful, Michael. It's not your usual mode-of-operation, and it's causin' you to miss somethin'—somethin' important."

Tentatively, he ventured, "Could you make any suggestions as to what I may have missed?"

She blew out a breath. "No—not really." She couldn't very well start speaking of vengeance-ghosts or bread-puddings, least she lose whatever remaining shred of credibility she had. "But I do know that Savoie's just as angry as you are." Remembering the Frenchman's rather pointed remark at the park, she added, "I think it has somethin' to do with Gemma."

Her husband admitted, "I was delaying Gemma's adoption, in an attempt to force his hand."

She glanced up at him in surprise. "Didn't much work, did it? I could have told you that."

"He does not respond in the usual fashion," her husband admitted.

She made a wry mouth. "Aye, that; he doesn't like anyone tellin' him what to do. There's some psychological reason—his childhood, or somethin'. He's a lot like you, in a way."

"I would disagree," Doyle's husband replied in an even tone.

Immediately backtracking, she assured him, "No, of course not —I was just teasin' you, my friend." Now, there was a misstep— not the right thing to say, lass; *try* to control your tongue, for the love o' Mike.

She tucked her hand in his arm, and they walked in silence for a few minutes until he said, "I should return to finish-up my meeting, if I may."

"Aye—I'm sorry, to have pulled you away, but I thought it was that important to let you know that you were pluckin' at the wrong bow-string. What's your meetin'?"

"I am meeting with the Crown Prosecutors about Howard's trial."

She glanced up; a bit surprised that he'd be involved. "You're not testifyin', are you?"

"I am not on the witness-list," he agreed.

Oh-oh, she thought, as she moved her hair away from Tommy's reaching grip. Pay attention, lass; I think your wily husband just gave you a non-answer. But—there would be no reason for Acton to testify at the trial, surely? The direct evidence from Howard's flat had disappeared, and so they were going to have to rely on the Coroner's testimony—that, and Lizzie's forensic analysis—to trace the batch of tainted medication into Howard's corpse. No reason, for the illustrious Chief Inspector to take the stand.

Suddenly, she was reminded of something the ghost had said —there's good reason, he doesn't want you there. Was the ghost referring to Howard's trial? And would the reason be because she'd know if untruths were being told?

She was pulled away from these troubling thoughts, when her husband asked, "May I drop you at St. Michael's?"

"No," she decided. "I need to go home and regroup with these children. I'll call Nellie, and push her back until tomorrow mornin'. If her bookkeeper's the Jane Doe at the morgue, she'll keep."

They turned to head toward the gate, with Doyle facing the rather disturbing realization that she'd even more spokes flying about than yesterday, but still no hub that held them all together.

CHAPTER 33

Doyle was unsurprised when Acton came home that evening to report that he could find no link to Savoie, in the circumstances of Sasha Lanska's death. "Not that I doubt you," he added immediately, because he was making up for his moment of doubt in the park.

"There's a link," she said thoughtfully. "Mark me."

Her husband pointed out reasonably, "If your theory is correct, and her death was intended as a message, then you would think he'd want to make it clear that it was he who was behind it."

"Oh, they got the message, all right," Doyle replied, thinking about Denisovich and Sir Vikili. "The poor geese are properly terrified."

Reminded, she added, "Note that Sir Vikili keeps showin' up every time we turn around. I still think that he's tryin' to warn you about somethin', without comin' straight out and sayin' what it is."

Acton crossed his arms, and gazed out the window at the night sky for a moment. "Perhaps he wished to hint that Savoie indeed killed Sasha, but he cannot betray his client by saying it aloud?"

She made a face. "I'm not buyin' it. Recall that Sir Vikili once tried to frame Savoie for murder."

"A very good point," he conceded.

She added, "And—come to think of it—Sir Vikili owes you one, over that particular little incident. He owes me, too, if we're keepin' score."

Acton nodded thoughtfully. "So; Sir Vikili is giving hints, but he is constrained in some way?"

"Aye—that sounds more like it. He's that fashed about somethin', and he needs you to save the day, but he can't tell you, straight-out, about whatever-it-is."

Thinking this over, Doyle offered, "Mayhap it has somethin' to do with the Persian community, instead of Sir Vikili in particular. When I was given the hint about Nazy's Kian, there was a reference made to that—to the community."

Acton would have guessed that it was Gabriel, who'd given her the hint, but she'd do her part to keep his name out of it. She added, "That might be what it is, that makes Sir Vikili tread so carefully. He can't betray Denisovich by sayin' why Savoie killed Sasha, because such a betrayal would reflect badly on the Persian community. After all, there's an ancient alliance, betwixt the Persians and the Russians."

Acton turned to regard her with no small surprise. "You astonish me, Lady Acton."

Airily, she replied, "Oh, I know a thing or two about ancient alliances—and ancient grudges, too. Recall that I hail from the Auld Sod."

He bowed his head, considering this. "So; Sir Vikili, who is Persian, cannot be seen as betraying the Russians."

"Somethin' like that," she agreed, her brow knit. "We need to know more."

He reminded her, "I'm not certain what that alliance would have to do with Savoie, though."

Doyle frowned. "Oh. Oh—you're right; I'm not sure how the two would tie together."

"Food for thought, though."

"Are you humorin' me?" she asked suspiciously. She hated it, when he humored her.

"No," he said, and it was the truth. "I would agree that there is something at play here that we do not understand."

"Yet," she added thoughtfully. "We will—I have it on good authority."

And, as though on cue, Doyle was once again visited by the ghost of Nigel Howard that night.

Almost immediately, she offered with some relief, "I think Acton's steppin' back from the ledge a bit."

"Yes," the ghost agreed. "Well done."

"I've no idea what I'm doin'," she confessed.

"You will; I have every confidence."

"Will I have to be brave?" Doyle ventured. "I'm pig-sick of bein' brave."

"No, no," he assured her. "Not you, this time."

"Well, that's a relief—although Savoie's mighty wary of me, and I don't know why."

The ghost pointed out, "Your allegiance is not to him."

This seemed a good point, and she reasoned, "I suppose that's true; he's actually wary of Acton, and so he can't trust me an inch, since I'm the man's wife. Faith, it's a shame that it's gotten to this."

"Pride," the ghost explained. "Which is another of the seven deadly sins. When you think about it, wrath is often a symptom of the deadly sin of pride."

"Their egos get in the way, she agreed. "Like Hector and Achilles; neither one could see that peace is its own reward—neither one even wanted to. They just wanted to win, and never mind the consequences."

"Hector is a good fellow," the ghost reminded her. "Ferocious, and loyal."

Doyle knit her brow. "I thought Raven was a good fellow."

The ghost smiled. "Raven is the best of good fellows."

Reminded of yet another discrepancy, she ventured, "I'm that flummoxed; Mary doesn't think you liked her bread-puddin', but you're not lyin' about it."

"It was our little secret," the ghost explained.

There was a small silence. "I can't make heads-nor-tails of any of this," Doyle admitted. "Even Acton is stumped, and he's not one who stumps easily."

"He won't be for long," the ghost assured her. "Thanks to you."

With a pang of compassion, she said suddenly, "You're such a kind man—so encouragin'—and it all seems so unfair. I had one of these dreams, once, and I saw Gemma goin' into her weddin'. I didn't think about it at the time, but you weren't there. It's such a shame—I'm that sorry, you're dead."

"I'm not sorry," the ghost replied, and smiled.

CHAPTER 34

$\mathcal{T}$he next morning, after Doyle got her household squared-away, she went down to the front pavement where Nellie swung by to pick her up, so as to take her over to the central London morgue. The Filipino woman was rather somber, and so the ride was quieter than their usual. This was to the good, though; it gave Doyle a chance to think about what the ghost had said the night before. She decided that she was getting a bit better at interpreting Howard-speak—a shame he was a diplomat, and therefore incapable of saying anything in plain terms.

In sum, it seemed that he wanted her to know that Acton had it wrong; her husband thought he was the fox, laying a wily trap for Savoie's gingerbread man, but instead the two men were actually Hector and Achilles, doomed to destroy each other—and a lot of other people, too—as a result of prideful wrath. And— here was the corker—someone else was having to be brave, for a change; it didn't fall to the fair Doyle.

In any event, the ghost had assured her that she was making headway—not that she hadn't sensed this, herself; Acton wasn't half so wound-up as he'd been on holiday—that state of affairs no doubt brought about because he'd truly believed that Savoie had killed Howard, and knew what a nightmare scenario this created. Not to mention Acton would be enraged that Savoie would dare do such a thing, and think he'd get clean away with it.

But now, slowly but surely, her husband was listening to her and unwinding—even if just a tiny bit. It was to the good; she needed that mind of his to be clear and unclouded so as to sort-out this puzzle.

Turning to the task at hand, Doyle asked Nellie, "Tell me what you know about our Mrs. Rossa. Mary seems to think she's from Eastern Europe, somewhere."

Nellie nodded. "Yes, Belarus. She was good with the accounts, but I don't know a lot because she tended to keep to herself. She was friendly with Mary though—she always offered to assist, when Mary came in to change the flowers every week."

Doyle smiled. "Not a surprise; everyone's friendly with Mary —it can't be helped."

"Very true." Nellie cast Doyle an arch look. "Father John thinks that Frenchman is going to marry her."

"I wouldn't bet against Father John, when it comes to predictin' such things." Best not to mention that Savoie could be indicted for a sensational murder at any moment, depending on how much faith Acton had in his wedded wife.

Doyle continued, "Did Mrs. Rossa belong to any groups, or have any hobbies? Mary says she was a baker."

Diplomatically, Nellie offered, "Yes—she did talk about baking, but I wondered if it was something she would say just to please Mary. She never brought-in anything for us to sample, and usually that's what bakers do."

"Aye, that," Doyle agreed, but decided that this didn't seem a very promising lead, and so she moved on to the next one. "Mary mentioned she attended the Russian Orthodox Church, here in town."

Again, Nellie used a diplomatic tone. "Yes. I didn't have the impression she was very religious, though."

Since Nellie was a true believer, she would know of which she spoke, and so Doyle mused, "An odd sort of person, then, if she's ROC, not very religious, but winds up workin' in an RC church."

"Theirs is an odd sort of church," Nellie replied, a bit tartly. Nellie was staunchly RC, and tended to regard any other denomination with a touch of suspicion. "Father John told me they held a consecration ceremony a few years back, to dedicate a martyr's altar to the Tsar's family. He said it was somewhat controversial, even within their own church, because the Tsar and his family weren't killed because of their faith. Father John doesn't think you can be a martyr unless you die in witness."

Doyle smiled. "Did Father John go over there, and give them a righteous piece of his mind?"

Nellie smiled in response. "Oh, no—he wouldn't dream of it; in fact, Father John invites their priest over for the ecumenical luncheon every year. He's a very nice man."

"Aye," Doyle agreed. "I met him once—I went over there, when I was supposed to attend Mary's weddin' to Nigel Howard."

Nellie turned to give her a surprised look. "Was Nigel Howard ROC?"

Oh-oh, thought Doyle; I probably should avoid any discussion of that particular runaway marriage, and the reasons for it. "Mayhap," she equivocated, and quickly changed the subject. "You should brace yourself, Nellie. I'd be very surprised if this Jane Doe wasn't poor Mrs. Rossa."

"I know," Nellie said quietly. "I still haven't been able to contact her, and so I think you must be right. Even if she returned to Belarus, she'd have said something—she was very reliable."

They parked, and made their way into the unassuming building, where Doyle greeted the same Coroner's Assistant that she'd met once before, on that memorable occasion when she'd discovered that the latest Thames drowning victim was, in fact, Lady Abby. "I came in last year, remember? Now, there was a corker."

"I remember, Officer Doyle," said the woman, with a small smile. "It was indeed a memorable visit."

Doyle explained to Nellie, "I wandered-in to check-out a potential homicide, all unknowin' that it would turn out to be someone I knew."

The Coroner's Assistant was understandably surprised. "Is this one a potential homicide, too? We didn't note any signs of foul play."

"No—not this time. Instead Nellie, here, has a church-bookkeeper who's gone missin', and this Jane Doe fills the bill. Nellie would like to see her properly buried, if it's indeed the same person."

The Assistant addressed Nellie, "I'm sorry for it, ma'am, but at the same time, I'm relieved. It's always so frustrating when we can't come up with an ID."

"No autopsy?" Doyle asked, as they turned to follow the Assistant through the security door and into the cold environs of the morgue.

"No. We leaned toward suicide, rather than misadventure." This was standard; if there was nothing to raise suspicion and no ID, the Coroner was unlikely to spend the money on an autopsy.

They walked along the double rows of drawers in the "unclaimed" portion of the facility, each drawer labeled with an identifying number. The Assistant paused before one of the drawers and then turned to Nellie. "Are you ready, ma'am? And if you don't feel well, we've a chair just over there."

"I'm ready," said Nellie, in her practical manner. "And I arrange for funerals at the church, so this will be nothing new."

With a solemn expression that befit the occasion, the young woman pulled the drawer out, and then carefully unzipped the body bag to expose the decedent's face.

"*Holy* Mother of God," Doyle exclaimed aloud, unable to stop herself. Because laid out before her was yet another spoke, in this unending wheel; the still, cold figure wasn't Nellie's bookkeeper at all, but was Miss Valerie, Doyle's erstwhile nanny.

CHAPTER 35

*I*n short order, Nellie had been dispatched home, and Doyle's husband now stood beside her, reviewing the nanny's remains, whilst the Coroner's Assistant was—yet again— being called upon to answer some very troubling questions as they were being directed toward her by the famed Chief Inspector.

She's holding up well, thought Doyle; much better than I used to, when I stood in her place.

"Who made the determination this was suicide, instead of misadventure?"

"I did, sir. There were no signs of trauma, and she's well-groomed."

This was a fair point; suicides tended to fit in two categories— those who killed themselves in a horrifying manner so as to send an accusing message to the person who would find them, or those who made certain the opposite was the case, so that their loved ones would not be overly-traumatized.

"And she has pin-point pupils, sir. It would be consistent with an opioid overdose."

Acton nodded, as he bent to lift an eyelid and see for himself. "Would you explain, please, why there was no attempt made to match her prints?" This, because all the nannies who'd been vetted by their fancy agency would have their fingerprints on public file.

Surprised, the woman replied, "But there was an effort, sir. I took her prints and ran them through the database, myself."

Doyle could see that this caught his interest, and he straightened up to cross his arms. "And they came up 'no match'—you are certain?"

"I may have mis-entered," the Assistant replied fairly. "But the results showed no match."

Acton ordered, "We will need an autopsy on an expedited basis as well as a toxicological investigation, please. Keep it quiet, if you would. And I would ask for a copy of her prints, to take with me now."

"Yes, sir."

"Sergeant," he said to Doyle. "I would like to confer."

"Yes, sir," Doyle replied, a bit startled, and duly noted that Acton had decided this was a homicide case—which was exactly what she thought, and so at least she wouldn't have to try and convince him.

They stepped across the hallway into the morgue's sad little waiting room, and he closed the door behind them. "Your thoughts, please."

Doyle blew out a breath. "It's a bit of a rabbit-hole—I'm givin' you fair warnin'."

He tilted his head. "Let's hear it."

"Our Miss Valerie was Eastern European, right?"

He regarded her, for a silent moment. "Yes, Valerie Cervena, originally from Czechoslovakia."

"There are people who keep disappearin', Michael, and it

seems that everyone who's disappearin' is either Slavic—like the bookkeeper, and Miss Valerie—or they're Persian. There was a Persian man who worked at the transport company for a bit, but he left between the time the fentanyl deaths broke, and before we opened a case. His supervisor readily admitted that he was a dosser—so she wasn't a'tall surprised that he didn't show up one day. But then, he never collected his wages owed. You'd think a dosser would be keen to collect his wages."

She paused, and Acton prompted, "Who else is Persian and has disappeared?"

"Oh—I forgot to tell you; Nazy's beau, Kian."

He raised his brows in surprise. "Kian has disappeared?"

"Aye. And poor Nazy's been tryin' to track him down, but with no luck."

He thought this over. "The church bookkeeper is Slavic?"

"Aye—she hails from Belarus. "And I also forgot to tell you that both she and Miss Valerie attended the same church—the Russian Orthodox one, here in town. Mrs. Mackey mentioned it to Mary, because she goes there too."

He allowed his skepticism to show. "If they are Slavic, attendance at that church may not be such a surprise, certainly?"

"Neither one seemed very religious, though."

But he continued skeptical. "It may have been more a desire to be amongst an expat community, Kathleen."

Stubborn, he is, thought Doyle; he doesn't want to leave go of the Savoie-is-the-villain storyline. "Well, I know there doesn't seem to be a rhyme nor a reason, but there does seem to be a pattern, here, startin' with Sasha."

Again, he allowed his skepticism to show. "I will point out that Sasha did not disappear. Nor did Miss Valerie."

But Doyle countered, "I will give you the point about Sasha, but Miss Valerie's as good as disappeared, Michael, if she's lyin' here under the wrong prints. Mayhap we should make certain that the John Does who are here, aren't actually Nazy's beau, or Ahmed, the transport fellow."

"An excellent suggestion," he agreed.

A half-hour later, they were in the car and driving back to headquarters, having determined that none of the anonymous John Does in the morgue fit the description of the missing Persian men.

Her husband was deep in thought, and—after leaving him to it for as long as she was able—Doyle ventured, "What are you thinkin'?"

Recalled from his abstraction, he told her, "I would very much like to know at what point the prints were switched, so as to hide Miss Valerie's true identity."

Doyle offered, "I doubt it was the morgue; the Coroner's Assistant seems to be on the up-and-up. I'm amazed you haven't recruited her, Michael—she seems very competent."

"I would agree."

"So; the prints were switched by Miss Valerie, herself?"

"Or the agency. It is a clever gambit, since it is unlikely anyone would cross-check for prints when a candidate shows up for an interview."

Doyle made a face. "Lesson learned, for the next time. Faith, it makes my blood run cold, to think that she was a wolf in sheep's clothin'. But what was the purpose? She's done nothin' to raise suspicion."

He replied, "I am not certain we can presume that her death was related to the deception."

But this seemed obvious, to Doyle, and so she glanced at him in puzzlement. "Why can't we can presume it?"

"If she had malicious intent, she was thwarted, and almost immediately."

The penny dropped, and Doyle could see his point. "If she's up to no good, then why would someone kill her just after she's managed to place herself in position? You're right—it doesn't make a lot of sense. Mayhap there's truly a turf-war, goin' forward —with the Russians and the Persians hardest hit. Mayhap hers was an admonishment-murder; a warnin' by whoever's on the other side to back off."

"Perhaps," he agreed. "Or there may be a simpler explanation; it may be that her deception was an attempt to hide from whoever wound-up killing her."

"Now, there's an idea," Doyle agreed. "I suppose that would make me feel a tiny bit less stupid—if she was just tryin' to hide-out, for some reason."

But after thinking about this for a minute, she slowly shook her head. "I don't think that's the case, Michael—I truly don't think she's the victim, here. Now that we know she was a fraud, it seems obvious that she wasn't a very good nanny—she'd no idea how to deal with a wild-child like our Edward. And why would anyone decide to hide-out as a nanny, for an aristocratic family? It would be a lot of trouble to take—not to mention that you'd be workin' for Lord Acton, who'd be very likely to catch you out. Why take that chance? I think instead we can conclude that she was up to no good."

But he pointed out reasonably, "If that were the case, she'd plenty of opportunity but didn't take it."

"Yet," Doyle stubbornly replied. "She was thwarted, for reasons unknown."

He nodded—being careful, he was, to cast no aspersions on his wedded wife's perceptive abilities due to the fact he'd got into trouble the day before. "Did you ever gain the impression that she was attempting to gather information from you?"

Thinking it over, Doyle slowly shook her head. "No—it would

have set-off alarm bells, I think, if she'd started askin' about anythin' other than ordinary nannyin' things."

She then paused, much struck. "You know, Williams said the same thing about Sasha—that it would have set off alarm bells, if she'd tried to probe for state secrets. He said Sasha made no such attempt—she only asked him about ordinary things."

"I am not yet certain we can presume the two deaths are related."

This was classic Acton, in that he wasn't a leaper-to-conclusions. His wedded wife, however, was a leaper like no other and she insisted, "I think they are, Michael—it can't be a coincidence." She glanced over at him. "Mayhap we should head over to the agency, and knock a few heads together."

But he cautioned, "Not as yet; I would like to keep this discovery quiet for the time being. Now that I have the true prints, I will first see what I can discover."

This made sense, and she nodded. "Aye, then. Let me know if you need me to do a little listenin'."

He checked his watch. "I'd rather you spare a few minutes—if you would—and speak with Nazy. I would like as much information as you can obtain about her beau, without unduly alarming her. Especially any known-associates he may have mentioned."

"I will," she agreed. "And I'll check-in with my other source, too—the one that I promised not to name."

"Only be careful what you say to him."

She nodded, because of course, Acton was keeping a wary eye on Gabriel-of-the-warnings. "I will."

CHAPTER 36

*U*nder the guise of showing a friendly concern, Doyle was trying to quiz Nazy about her erstwhile beau but she was finding it slow-going, mainly because the young woman was emanating waves of misery, and wasn't particularly eager to probe that wound.

"Mayhap the boyo has amnesia," Doyle suggested. "He's in hospital, languishin' away, and no one knows. Did he have any family in the area?"

"That's just it, Officer Doyle. He was going to bring me to meet his parents—he kept talking about it. He told me his father had a shop in Bayswater." With a conscious air, she confessed, "I walked the whole street, but I couldn't find a single shopkeeper with his name."

"Oh," said Doyle. "Well, that's a bit discouragin'." She then tried to decide if there was any way she could ask Nazy if she had any objects with her beau's fingerprints, without sounding a bit crazed.

"I wish I knew what happened," the girl continued in a subdued tone. "I just want to hear an explanation."

"If only we knew how to get hold of him," Doyle agreed. "D'you remember his mentionin' any friends? Classmates, from school?"

But Nazy only shook her head. "I did wonder if he might come to Mr. Howard's murder trial. He was very upset about what happened."

Doyle slid her gaze over to the girl. "Spoke of it often, did he?"

"Oh, yes."

"Is anyone that he knows goin' to testify? Anyone from his security desk?"

"No—I don't think so. He did know someone over at Griffin Transport, though—the place where that whistleblower was killed."

"Oh, yes," Doyle said, in a casual tone. "There was a Persian fellow workin' there, named Ahmed Tehrani. Was that the friend?"

"I don't remember the name," Nazy admitted. With a touch of forlorn hope, she brightened. "But I wonder if Ahmed would know how to contact Kian?"

Nobody's going to be contacting either one of them, thought Doyle, a bit grimly, but instead she asked, "Can you think of anyone else? Did he belong to any groups?"

"No—I don't think so."

"Did he mention any relatives, other than his parents?"

"No—except Sir Vikili, of course." She paused, suddenly struck. "I wonder if Kian will go to his wedding?"

Hastily, Doyle pointed out, "It's probably not good form to crash Sir Vikili's weddin', Nazy, and cause a scene with one of his guests. The Chief Inspector would be that annoyed with you."

Ashamed, the girl ducked her head. "I know, Officer Doyle. You must think I'm pathetic."

"Not a'tall," Doyle rallied her. "Kian wasn't a good man, Nazy, to do this to you, and therefore you should thank God fastin' that you've had such a lucky escape."

"Yes, I know," the girl agreed, but—in the manner of the yearning heartbroken—this sentiment wasn't exactly true.

Thoughtfully, Doyle was making her way over to Officer Gabriel's office, when her phone pinged, and the ID showed that it was Mary. "Ho, Mary."

"I'm sorry to bother you, Lady Acton, but would you mind if I dropped-off Gemma for a bit, later this afternoon? Callie's visiting her folks, and Mrs. Mackey has offered to sit Hannah, but I'd feel better if she only had to mind the baby. I have to go meet with the prosecutors about the trial."

Doyle assured her, "Of course, Mary—Reynolds will love a visit with Gemma. And I'll come along with you to meet with the prosecutors—happy to do it."

"No—thank you, though. Philippe's coming, along with his solicitor." She lowered her voice. "His solicitor is quite fearsome; I think he makes everyone nervous."

Doyle smiled into the phone. "He's not the only one. Between Savoie and Sir Vikili, you'll be well looked-after. Just ping me when Gemma's in the lobby, and I'll have Reynolds go down to fetch her."

"Thank you so much, Lady Acton."

Doyle sheathed her phone and then poked her head into Gabriel's open office door. "Have a mo?"

The young man looked up, and readily waved her in. "Of course; you're my favorite Countess. What's up?"

Carefully, she closed the door behind her and then leaned against it. "I don't have all day, because I'm not goin' to let my poor baby go hungry again. Therefore, I'd appreciate it if you will tell me what you know with no roundaboutation."

He eyed her, and replied a bit cautiously, "I know a lot of things. Which, in particular?"

Doyle decided to cut to the nub. "About why Persian people are disappearin', including the dodgy boyfriend that you warned me about."

There was a long moment whilst he regarded her thoughtfully. "I do have a theory, but you didn't hear it from me."

"Fair enough; now, spill."

"The disappearing Persian people are being murdered."

She made a sound of derision. "Are they? Mother a' Mercy—stop the presses."

He lifted his brows. "Not good enough?"

"No. And let's start with why Sir Vikili is droppin' hints about these victims. That's not his style, at all."

Gabriel leaned back in his chair and contemplated the ceiling for a moment. "I can't be certain, because the man doesn't confide in me, but I would guess he's worried that he's on the list of Persian people to be killed."

She stared at him, agog. "Faith, Gabriel; who'd dare kill Sir Vikili?"

"I do have a theory."

Impatiently Doyle urged, "Then let's hear it, for heaven's sake; I've a hungry baby at home and I'm half-ready to put you on that list, myself."

Coming to a decision, he met her eyes. "Philippe Savoie."

Doyle stared at him. "*What?*"

With a touch of amusement, he noted, "There; that little tidbit garnered a much better reaction."

With no small astonishment, she repeated, "You think it was *Savoie*, who's been killin' these Persians?"

"Yes. I would assume so."

This was true, and she frowned at him. "Why? And why would he go after Sir Vikili? The man's worth his weight in gold, as a solicitor." Belatedly, she remembered to add, "Hence."

Her companion shrugged. "I don't know the motivation behind it, but that's my best guess."

Thoroughly confused, Doyle stared at him, and was immediately reminded that she held the certain conviction that Savoie had killed Sasha Lanska, too. But how was that murder related to these ones? The only link, it seemed, was the famous Persian solicitor.

She was also reminded that Savoie was suddenly bringing security with him, even to the park. "Holy *Mother*, Gabriel—did Sir Vikili double-cross Savoie?" She paused, much struck. "Although I suppose it wouldn't be much of a surprise—he's done so, before."

This was of interest, and Gabriel raised his brows. "Has he?"

Hastily, Doyle buttoned her lip—she'd been doing so well, and then she'd slipped up. "Never you mind; instead, tell me why you think this."

Choosing his words, her companion observed, "It appears that Savoie is engaged in an all-out campaign to cover his tracks."

Oh-oh, thought Doyle, who was reminded that her wedded husband shared some of those self-same tracks. "What's he tryin' to cover-up? It must be a corker, if Sir Vikili thinks this is the final straw, and Savoie's comin' after him."

But Gabriel hesitated, and cocked a brow at her. "The Chief Inspector hasn't made mention?"

Doyle confessed, "I tend to gabble, so Acton doesn't always tell me things." But in truth, Gabriel's question was actually a massive relief; Gabriel was hinting that Acton was fully-aware of whatever

Savoie was up to, and so it seemed unlikely that there was any danger that the Chief Inspector would be implicated in the aforesaid covering-of-tracks. Acton was the grand master at damage control, in the same way he was the grand master at turning the tables.

Her scalp started prickling and she paused, wondering why it would. What? If she'd learned nothing else in her marriage to the man, she'd learned that Acton loved nothing better than turning the tables back on the villains—especially villains who'd tried to bring him down. It was something of a failing, but there it was; he loved outfoxing his enemies in the same way his ancestors had done for nearly a thousand years. Vengeance was in his blood, along with wrath, and pride, and all those other very questionable medieval urges.

Her scalp prickled yet again, and as she frowned in distraction Gabriel continued, "I will agree that being a gabbler is part of your charm. However, it does make me hesitate to unburden myself to you."

"You should," she insisted. "I'll fall on my sword rather than grass you out, and I think it's important."

"You do have good instincts," he mused, as though debating what to do.

"Spill," she pleaded. "Sir Vikili's finally got a chance at happiness, and that's why he's so very fashed."

She was surprised she'd said such a thing, and—reading the other's expression—so was Gabriel, apparently. Nonetheless, the remark seemed to turn the trick, and he leaned forward to offer in a low tone, "I hear rumor that Savoie burned down the coin shop in Bristol so as to destroy evidence. A field officer had gone in—some weeks ago—on a burglary investigation and wound up seizing a cache of fentanyl from the shop's safe."

Doyle made a sound of impatience. "I think everyone with half a brain-cell knew that coin shop was involved in dodgy dealings, Gabriel."

Carefully, he continued, "There is some speculation that the fentanyl seized from the coin shop was from the tainted lot."

Very much surprised, she stared at him for a moment. "So; there's hard evidence that Savoie was involved in the drug-murders?"

Her companion nodded. "They're keeping it very quiet, of course. He's a flight risk."

"Holy *Mother*, Gabriel."

"I tend to agree."

In abject surprise, she lowered her gaze to the floor. Hard as it was to believe, Acton was right, and her instinct was wrong. Philippe Savoie had ruthlessly murdered Nigel Howard, and Doyle's husband hadn't wanted to tell her about this latest, damning piece of evidence because it had the tightest of lids on it —Savoie was slippery as an eel, with a long history of evading law enforcement.

Mother a' Mercy, but she'd been on the wrong track, and suddenly it all made sense; Acton was taking-down Savoie, which would save Mary from marrying her husband's killer—it would save Mary, just as the ghost wanted. It all made perfect sense. Except, of course, that it didn't.

With a mighty effort, Doyle pulled herself together and lifted her gaze to her companion. "Savoie's not a defendant in the homicide case, though. Are they lullin' him into thinkin' he's off the hook?"

"It would seem so."

Bewildered, she raised her palms. "But how can the prosecution keep this a secret? All evidence has to be shared with the defense."

Gabriel pointed out, "They don't have to share it, if it's going to be used as impeachment evidence—to show that a witness is lying on the stand. Which is why—I imagine—the prosecution is planning to present the coin shop evidence as impeachment evidence."

The light suddenly dawned, and Doyle reasoned, "And any impeachment witnesses don't have to be on the witness-list, either. There's no requirement to tell the defense about them ahead of time."

He nodded. "Correct. It's a clever way to get Savoie's involvement into the record, without tipping him off ahead of time."

"Indeed, it is." Doyle agreed, her tone slightly grim. "As clever as a fox. And Savoie's goin' to attend the trial, which means he'll have to go through a metal detector to get into the courtroom. It would be a cinch, to arrest him the moment this evidence is revealed."

"You didn't hear it from me," Gabriel emphasized. "I'd rather not be the next disappearance on the list."

With all sincerity, she assured him, "I won't say a thing, my friend. And I owe you one."

"We're even," he reminded her, as he rose to get the door. "You saved me, once."

"Twice," she corrected. "Not that we're countin'."

CHAPTER 37

*A*lmost immediately, Doyle was on the phone. "Husband, would you mind droppin' me home? Can you spare a few?"

"What's happened?" he asked immediately. Acton had a fine-tuned radar, when it came to his wife.

"Nothin' dire; I just need to speak with you, is all." She paused. "Sooner, rather than later."

He confessed, "I am due for a final meeting with the prosecutor."

I'll bet you are, she thought. "It won't take long, I promise. Mayhap you could push them back."

There was a small pause, whilst her husband contemplated this rather extraordinary request—the Crown Prosecutors weren't people who liked to be pushed back when they were getting their ducks in a row for a sensational murder trial. "Right, then. Shall I meet you at the garage, or pick you up out front?"

"Out front," she decided. "See you there."

Letting out a long breath, Doyle began to make her way down

the hallway. There's good reason he doesn't want you there, the ghost had told her. Good reason, because if the fair Doyle attended Howard's murder-trial she'd know that her wily husband, the impeachment witness, would be giving false testimony so as to frame-up Savoie. The damning fentanyl evidence must have been planted by Trenton, when he'd been doing his mysterious Bristol sting-operation, some weeks ago. It would be a simple thing, actually, since Acton loyalist Lizzie Williams had been working in the forensics lab when the pertinent batch of tainted pills had gone mysteriously missing.

And—no doubt—it was also Trenton who'd burned the shop down. That was why the man hadn't gone on holiday with them; he was setting-up this Savoie-trap, and he'd been probably meeting-up with Acton when her husband had gone walking, at night.

Don't overreact, lass, she cautioned herself, because—in all fairness—Acton wasn't overreacting. Instead, he was behaving true-to-form; the man truly believed that Savoie should pay an epic price for such an epic crime, and so he was arranging for vengeance in true Acton-fashion. And who better to take-down Savoie than Acton? He'd know every flaw in Savoie's armor, and could gather-up false evidence against the man at the drop of a hat. The only fly in the epic ointment was the man's troublesome wife, and her sure sense that he was on the wrong track.

Doyle emerged onto the front pavement and lifted her face, so as to feel the weak sunlight. Mary needed saving, the ghost had said, and—ironically—it was the exact same situation as when the fair Doyle had saved Howard; it was Acton who she needed saving from. Acton, who was carefully planning Savoie's downfall, unaware that he would be making everything miles worse.

Frowning slightly, she was suddenly aware that if her trusty instinct was right—that Acton was about to make an epic blunder —then she still hadn't caught sight of the truth; the hub, that held it all together.

People were disappearing, and Sir Vikili was nervous enough to drop a warning to Acton about it. And Gabriel—who knew a thing or two, lest we forget—seemed to think that Savoie was the one who was making people disappear. Although Sasha hadn't disappeared, Savoie had left her burnt body as a grisly message— mayhap, a message to the dead woman's ex-husband? But all these others victims were simply being eliminated without a trace. Why?

Briefly, Doyle closed her eyes, but couldn't catch a glimpse of whatever-it-was that was motivating the Frenchman to go scorched-earth. You'll get there, the ghost had said, but at present, she didn't feel as though she was anywhere on the map.

Acton pulled up, and reached to open her door. As she slid in, she immediately, advised, "I don't blame you a'tall, Michael. Let's get that out of the way."

He was understandably made wary by this remark, and asked, "What did Nazy say?"

Impatiently, she advised, "I'll tell you in a mo, but first I have to tell you that you're barkin' up the wrong tree. You're plannin' to frame-up Savoie, and I know it looks bad, but Savoie didn't kill Howard."

There was a small pause. "Why do you think I am framing-up Savoie?"

"I'd rather not say."

Her husband was no fool, of course, and would know that she was hotfooting-it directly from Gabriel's office, but at a bare minimum she'd keep her promise. Hopefully, Acton would realize she'd be very unhappy if he took Gabriel to task for spilling the beans.

She repeated, "Savoie didn't kill Howard, Michael—my hand on my heart."

Rather than ask how she could be so certain—her husband had learned his lesson, the last time—instead, he reminded her, "You've said yourself, that the named defendants aren't clever enough for this fentanyl scheme, and the person behind it must have slipped the net."

"Aye," she agreed. "But it's not Savoie. I don't know who was behind it—there's somethin' here that we don't understand."

He was silent for a few moments, and then he asked, "What did Nazy say?"

"Nothin' of interest, save that Kian was a known-associate of Ahmed from Griffin Transport—the fellow who left work rather suspiciously."

Acton nodded. "I have also learned that Kian was receiving a healthy portion of Denisovich's alimony payments, every month."

She turned to him in surprise. "*Sasha* was funnelin' money to Kian? That can't be a coincidence, Michael; Kian's gettin' paid, he was on-site, and he had access to Howard's flat. He must have delivered the poison."

"I think that would be the working-theory."

Frowning, she stared at him. "Why on earth would *Sasha* want to kill Howard?"

"I think you are forgetting that Denisovich is affiliated with Savoie, Kathleen. By using Denisovich's wife to pay Kian, Savoie would have three cut-outs to separate him from the actual poisoning—Denisovich, Sasha, and Kian."

But Doyle only shook her head. "I think that only proves my point, Michael; your theory is flawed six ways to Sunday because Savoie's not one to trust anybody—especially this dodgy bunch."

Her husband glanced over at her. "Sasha is dead, Kian is dead

—we can presume—and Denisovich is worried that the same fate awaits him."

This was a fair argument, and—truth to tell—it did seem a good one. Slowly, she reasoned, "So; you think Savoie's erasin' anyone who could possibly grass on him, and that's why these people are disappearin'? Faith, but that's cold-blooded."

"Yes. But he had a compelling motive for his actions."

"Because he wanted Mary for himself."

He nodded. "You must admit, it is a sound working-theory."

"Aye," Doyle admitted fairly. "But it's the wrong one, and I'd feel miles better if I could figure out what Sasha's motive was, in paying Kian to poison Howard. I can't make heads nor tails."

Understandably nonplussed, her husband was silent for a moment. "You may be mistaken, Kathleen."

She knit her brow. "I don't think I am. I will grant you it looks mighty bad for Savoie, but that's part of the problem, here. You've put together a crackin' good frame-up because you're bound and determined to make him pay for his sins. But you're brimful of wrath, Michael, and it's blindin' your judgment."

He was silent for a few moments. "Why do you think this?"

"Your Savoie-theory doesn't explain why Denisovich divorced his beloved Sasha, and why her horribly-burnt corpse is the only one we see on full display. Faith, Michael, that's an admonishment-murder, if ever I saw one."

Thinking about this, Doyle frowned out the windscreen. "We're back to wonderin' what happened about three years ago, that made them set-up a sham divorce so as to funnel money to Howard's killers."

"So; your theory is that Denisovich wished to murder Howard?"

"No—I think it was Sasha, and he just went along. He loved her madly, after all, and remember I'd the sense he was very unhappy to be sittin' there, with you breathin' down his neck, on somethin' that wasn't his concern. I think she was the strong one, in that relationship—just like that dreadful woman from that Scottish play."

He remained silent, and she added, "And your Savoie-theory doesn't explain why Sasha was cat-fishin' Williams, or why Kian was cat-fishin' Nazy. Savoie would *never* have trusted any of these people to winkle-out information for him."

Carefully, she didn't add the obvious fact that her husband should have realized this without the wife of his bosom pointing it out. Which meant that Acton didn't much care about how all the details didn't seem to be adding up, because he had a prime opportunity to take-down Savoie and he was hell-bent on not wasting it. The prideful sin of wrath, on full display.

Her husband finally replied, "You make good points, Kathleen, but I will, in turn, point out we have no indication the motives for these—these catfishing expeditions—are related to the disappearances. There is no obvious link."

But she only gave him a look. "That's a coincidence too far, my friend. Kian *must* have been the one who planted the poisoned pills—he had the opportunity. We also know the likes of Savoie would *never* have trusted a chouser like Kian to murder *anyone* for him—not in a *million* years. And meanwhile, Kian is being well-paid by Sasha, who's another one Savoie would never have trusted in a million years."

They turned onto their street, and Acton was silent. He's that annoyed, she realized; for the first time ever, my husband's annoyed that I'm putting two-and-two together like a house afire.

In a conciliatory tone, she offered, "You don't want to hear it, because you'd be happy to lock-up our Mr. Savoie and throw away the key—no matter if he was behind Howard's murder or not."

He pulled in front of their building, and held up a hand to the approaching valet so as to stay him. Slowly, he admitted, "I suppose that is an accurate assessment."

Gently, she ventured, "I thought you'd promised Savoie that you'd not go after him, Michael."

"This would be the exception," he replied a bit too quickly. "Surely, you can see this."

She reached to take his hand, and say with all sincerity, "Small wonder, you're that fashed, Michael. It's not every day you break your word."

"The circumstances would warrant," he repeated, his gaze on her hand. "I have no qualms about it."

This was not true, and so she offered gently, "I know you're that annoyed with Savoie, and you've gone to a lot of effort, here, to get the whip-hand over him. But you've got to stop pushin' chests with the man, because there's somethin' else, here, and it's brewin' big, whatever it is."

His ducked his head for a moment. "I will admit your points are good ones. And that Miss Valerie's death is not easily explained."

Doyle blinked, having forgot about this little loose end. "Aye; she's an outlier, isn't she? She's not been disappeared, but on the other hand, she wasn't easy to find, so we can presume there was no message bein' sent, like there was with Sasha."

"Yes." He glanced over at her. "The preliminary tox screen shows fentanyl poisoning."

"Does it? I'm almost not surprised." She shook her head in wonder. "Mother a' Mercy, but this is a full-on rabbit maze and I can't fathom any of it. Could we get Savoie to answer your questions, somehow, with me listenin' in?"

He tilted his head. "It is unlikely he would speak of it under any circumstances, Kathleen. And I doubt he'd even take my call."

She made a face. "Nor mine; he doesn't trust either one of us, just now, and small blame to him if he suspects that it's you who's burnt-down the coin shop. But we have to fix this, somehow; you've got to leave go of your wrath, Michael, and instead be an Isaac. In the epic tales it's always the hero's own ego that destroys him. Leave go of your wrath, and be an Isaac."

"Excellent advice," he replied, and it was not exactly true.

"Let me know if you need me to help," she urged.

"I will. I must go."

He signaled to the valet, who promptly hurried over to open her door.

"See you later," she said cheerfully, just so the valet didn't think they'd been quarreling.

And now, she thought, as she watched him drive away; we will see how much faith my husband has in me.

CHAPTER 38

*D*espite all the various unsettling events which were going forward, Doyle had children to see to, and it was just as well; there was little time to think about murders and epic betrayals when one was breastfeeding a baby whilst listening attentively to a rambling toddler.

And she was to gain further distraction when the Concierge rang up, to announce that Gemma was in the lobby. Naturally, Doyle had forgot that the girl was coming, and thus had excused Reynolds to run a few errands during nap time.

"Oh—oh right; would you mind bringin' her up? And don't ring, just tap quietly."

With ruthless efficiency, Doyle put Edward down for his nap—he'd never sleep, if he knew Gemma was there—and then hurried back upstairs, just in time to answer the front door.

"Hallo, Gemma," Doyle greeted the little girl, and then took her jacket, to hang in the hall closet. "It's just you and me, today—"

She paused in astonishment, because this was not exactly true.

Across Doyle's main room walked the same ghost-dog who'd been at the park. Again, the dog showed little interest in Doyle—or anything else, for that matter—and instead, he padded over to the windows and lay down.

With a mighty effort, Doyle drew her attention back to Gemma, who'd gone over to coo at baby Tommy where he was parked on the sofa. "Help me put him down, Gemma, and then we can start an art project—I know just the thing."

In short order, Doyle was seated at the kitchen table with Gemma as the little girl went through Edward's stash of seashells, choosing the ones she liked in particular. "I'll glue them to a card, for my mum—and one for Hannah, too."

"Now, there's a good idea, Gemma. And I think we've some glitter in the box; you can't make a decent seashell-card without a dash of glitter."

The little girl smiled, and bent over the table so as to concentrate on the project.

Look at me, handling three children at a time and with no reinforcements whatsoever, thought Doyle; along with a ghost-dog—although he doesn't seem to be much trouble. She was mentally patting herself on the back for a job well done when Gemma's voice interrupted her thoughts.

As the girl carefully pressed a seashell onto the piece of art-paper, she asked, "Is that your dog, Lady Acton?"

Doyle stared at the girl's bent head for a long moment, and then managed to find her voice. "No, lass—I never had a dog. I think—I think he was your papa's."

Gemma paused to consider this, her brow furrowed. "Is his name 'Raven'? Papa used to keep his collar in his top drawer."

Doyle said softly, "Aye; that's the one."

Gemma smiled slightly, and addressed the shell-work again,

seemingly unmoved by the fact there was a ghost-dog following her about.

And this should be a lesson to me, thought Doyle in some bemusement; I'm always that fashed about the stupid ghosts—although it's a bit different, I suppose, since I'm expected to sort-out whatever jumbled message they're trying to relay to me.

Suddenly, she stilled. "Gemma," she asked. "Did your papa like bread-puddin'?"

Gemma glanced up, surprised, and then lowered her voice to a whisper. "It was a secret, Lady Acton; he didn't want my mum to know."

With dawning horror, Doyle stared at her. "Did he—did he used to sneak some of your bread-puddin' for his own lunch?"

A bit stricken at being thus found-out, the girl nodded. "Yes—I let him take the Friday muffin, each week." She ventured, "Did papa tell you, Lady Acton?"

"Indeed, he did," said Doyle, and found that her throat had closed with emotion. She'd been so blind—faith, they'd all been blind; this wasn't a turf-war, or anything as paltry as a falling-out amongst thieves. Instead, it was an ancient grudge—one that still festered, savage and unforgiving. The deadly sin of wrath—thriving, in this fallen world, with the full force of its fury directed toward this little girl. A little girl who was busy shaking glitter onto sea shells, and unaware of the cataclysmic events that she'd set off just by being born.

The Bolsheviks, Acton had called them. Or what remained of them, anyway—in the same way that Gemma was what remained of the Romanovs, and thus must be destroyed. The same way that the girl's parents had been destroyed before her lucky escape.

Doyle closed her eyes, briefly, as it all became clear. The perpetrators couldn't make their aim obvious, of course; after all, the girl's stepfather was an MP, and was tight-as-a-tick with the famous Chief Inspector. They'd need a foolproof plan, and therefore, an over-the-counter pain medication had been tainted with fentanyl, so that other people would die at the same time. Nine other people had been poisoned, to erase this living embodiment of their hated enemy.

The conspirators would need to find out what Gemma ate that no one else did—faith, Doyle had once been the subject of a similar plot, involving frosty flakes. And so probing questions had been asked of anyone who had access, with the church bookkeeper coming up with the needed information about the weekly muffin-tin of bread-puddings.

Once that information had been gleaned, Nazy's beau—who had access—would plant the fentanyl overdose into one of the muffins, and then empty the pills from a bottle of Howard's pain medication. The obvious conclusion would be that the little girl had got into her father's medicine, with her death just another sad tragedy amongst the other nine.

But the scheme hadn't worked. It hadn't worked, because no one knew that Howard would sneak the poisoned muffin to work with him, and would die as a result. Indeed, Howard's ghost kept saying he wasn't sorry that he was dead; he wasn't sorry, because it was a blessing that he was the one who'd died, instead of his little girl. In all things, give thanks.

And Savoie—Savoie must have found out, somehow; mayhap word had leaked, to the loyal Russians who worked for him? And so, the Frenchman was now in the process of laying terrible waste to all of the plotters. It wasn't his fight, but he'd made it his fight, because he was equal parts loyal and ferocious, and the villains, in this instance, had crossed the wrong watchdog.

It all fit in with the ghost's message; the last thing Howard would want was for Acton to go after Savoie, because—until these people were utterly destroyed—Gemma would be at risk. And if

Gemma were to be killed, Mary would be devastated. Avenge my death, the ghost had asked Doyle, because Acton was so blinded by wrath that he was focused like a laser-beam on the wrong suspect.

"I've got to phone my husband," Doyle said to Gemma. "I'll be right back."

CHAPTER 39

ortunately, Doyle didn't have to ask her husband to snub the Crown Prosecutors for the second time in a day, because his meeting had already adjourned by the time she called him, and he was on his way home.

"Kathleen," he said.

"Never mind that," she said abruptly. "Come straight up; hopefully Reynolds will be back soon and we can lock ourselves in your office. I've a debriefin' that will curl your hair."

"What has happened?" he asked, immediately on high alert.

"It can keep," she advised. "But don't make another move till you hear it. Promise me."

"Certainly. I will call Reynolds, and ask him to return immediately."

Reminded, Doyle advised, "Tell him no one comes in or out without your say-so. Tell Trenton, too."

There was a pause. "You alarm me."

This was not surprising, since the poor man's wife was sounding a bit crazed. To reassure him, she took a breath to calm herself down, and advised, "I think the time for bein' alarmed has passed, Michael. But best be safe."

And so, in short order, Doyle was standing with her husband in his home office—with Reynolds having taken over all seashell-gluing duties—and was reciting her conclusions to her husband whilst he listened intently.

"And so, all the while it was Gemma they were after, Michael. That's what happened, about three years ago—Gemma surfaced, and her identity was revealed. And so the divorce—and Sasha's withdrawin' from her political group—was just to cover-up their true intent; another assassination in their long and wrathful list of them. But no one knew that Howard sneaked the occasional bread-puddin', and so the plan went awry."

"Rasputin's honey-cakes," he said. "Yes."

Impatiently, she continued, "What*ever*, Michael; and I'll guess that the 'good' Russians who worked for Savoie, grassed-out the 'bad' Russians. It all fits; they must have given him the head's-up, because Savoie planted a new employee at Griffin Transport just after the murder, and the plant must have ferreted-out the people who'd been involved."

"Yes," he agreed, and met her eyes. "This is exceptional work, Kathleen."

She added, "If I were guessin', I'd guess that Sasha was the mastermind behind it—she was the true believer, not to mention that she was the one who took the brunt of Savoie's wrath."

"Yes," he agreed. "And poison tends to be a woman's weapon."

Slowly, Doyle shook her head in horrified amazement. "Faith, it's *awful*, Michael. What sort of woman would concoct such a plot against an innocent child?"

"A ruthless one," he replied. "I'd never met her, but it seems she had quite a forceful personality. And recall that much of her public persona stemmed from her politics; it was thought she may have been playing it up for the press, but it appears she was sincere."

"And it also explains why she was catfishin' Williams. He said she was askin' him about ordinary things—what Lizzie liked to bake for him."

He nodded. "Yes; Lizzie was cooking for the Howards at the time. And no doubt Miss Valerie came into our home, hoping to glean similar information; it was no secret, that our families were close."

Doyle closed her eyes, briefly. "It boggles the mind, Michael —*such* terrible people, with Sasha at the helm. She must have been funnelin' her fake-alimony to all of the conspirators—it only makes sense; Ahmed's supervisor said he was a dosser and he didn't seem to be much worried about keepin' his job."

Acton crossed his arms. "Did she indeed? And yet Ahmed wasn't named, when she was voicing her suspicions to the authorities. Even though he'd disappeared at the crucial juncture."

Doyle stared at him. "Now, there's a very good point."

"What was the supervisor's ethnicity?"

"I don't know, exactly," she admitted. "She was a One." This, referring to the police code that identified a Caucasian.

"What was your sense, when you were speaking with her?"

Doyle knit her brow, trying to remember. "A bit brassy. Joked about, askin' Williams if she could have a job—flirtin' with him, she was."

He turned to stare thoughtfully out the window, and Doyle ventured, "Should we go over there and rattle her cage, a bit?"

"No," he advised. "Better that she doesn't know we are suspicious."

"But the trial starts day after next, Michael, lest we forget— although I suppose it has to be postponed now. The prosecution has to be told that the case has gone in a different direction." With a full measure of misgiving, she added, "Not to mention that the prosecution will have to disclose *all* of this to the defense—Holy Mother, but it will be a crackin' firestorm."

But her husband only returned this thoughtful gaze to Doyle. "What would be the result, if I told the prosecutors who was actually behind Howard's death, and what their motivation was?"

"Misery for Mary," Doyle admitted. "More misery, heaped atop the last miserable misery."

"And notoriety, for Gemma. It would follow her the whole of her life."

Reluctantly, Doyle could only agree, even though she could see where he was going with this. "Aye."

In the manner of someone coming to an easy decision, he concluded, "Best leave it alone."

"But—but, innocent people might go to *prison*, Michael."

In a serious tone, he met her eyes. "No one is innocent in this, Kathleen. The true motive may have been obscured, but all the defendants are conspirators to murder. The theory still holds together—that they were after Howard for his role in taking-down the Public Accounts Commission."

It was the same old song—and long a point of contention between them. Acton thought nothing of arranging justice to suit his own notions, and Doyle could not be comfortable with such a misuse of authority. The system had been put in place so that the people who wielded power—like Acton, and his ancestors— weren't allowed to ride roughshod over everyone else. In this instance, though, it was hard to argue with this particular rough-shodding, even as she was aware that the minute you talked yourself into allowing exceptions, the whole system failed.

"I'd like to attend the trial," she said, a bit firmly. Best keep a wary eye on her wily husband; she'd the strong feeling he was cooking-up a plan—she knew the signs.

"By all means," he agreed.

But his mild tone only raised her suspicions, and so she prompted, "Tell me, here and now, that you've abandoned this fine opportunity to frame-up Savoie."

"I will not frame-up Savoie," he assured her, and it was the truth. "Quite the opposite, in fact."

At this remark, she made a wry mouth. "Naturally. And don't think that I'm fooled in the least by your mild-as-milk act, husband. You're that jealous that it wasn't you who's been layin' waste to all the evildoers."

He demurred, "Not at all; I am content to stand back in this instance. Please remember that I did so on another occasion, when Savoie moved to protect Gemma."

This version of events was not exactly true, as Doyle well-knew; on the last occasion, when Savoie had moved to protect Gemma, the Frenchman had done so in a way that had tied Acton's hands, and Acton wasn't one who liked having his hands tied. Indeed, she'd the sense that this was what had started the quarrel between the two.

Diplomatically, she replied, "Well—be that as it may—that occasion was nothin' like this one, you must admit. This one is just your style—Book of Revelation, fiery-lava-lakes level stuff. That's why Denisovich is so worried—and Sir Vikili, too. Savoie's brimful of wrath, and everyone's runnin' for cover."

"Very similar to King David at Ziklag, as a matter of fact."

There was a small pause, whilst Doyle couldn't help but smile. "Touché, husband. Which must mean that Savoie's no longer in your black book."

"I do not have a black book," he disclaimed.

But she made a skeptical sound. "Of course, you do; nursin' grievances is the only thing that keeps the nobs motivated."

Her husband smiled slightly, but added, "I will say that if Savoie has any claim to my black book, it is because he should have told me about this."

She raised her palms. "Faith, can you blame him? The both of you were pullin' caps, and he couldn't be sure you weren't lookin' for any excuse so as to pounce on him."

This, of course, was nothing less than the truth—although she probably shouldn't have pointed it out so bluntly—and so, she quickly added, "And he's a different sort of bird, Michael; he doesn't trust anyone—save Mary, apparently. Which is its own testament to the amazin' power of love."

He tilted his head. "I am not certain that Savoie is capable of such, Kathleen."

"There are plenty of people who would have said the same thing about you, my friend."

He smiled in amused acknowledgement. "Touché, right back."

There was a small silence, and—a bit warily—she asked, "So; what happens, now?"

But he met her eyes, his expression one of mild surprise. "Surely, you can see that it would be best to leave things lie? Those in need of punishment have been thoroughly punished; therefore, I will step away, and be an Isaac—just as you wish."

With a sigh, she noted, "I think you may be missin' the whole point of that story, Michael."

CHAPTER 40

The sensational trial was set to commence, and every available seat in the courtroom was taken; the atmosphere filled with the electric subcurrent of anticipation that always marked a notorious criminal trial. It was one of the few instances in real life where the audience was guaranteed to witness a slice of high drama, with the defendants' future hanging in the balance.

Doyle sat stoically in the first row, next to her husband. She never enjoyed crowds—it was never comfortable, for her, to sense multiple cross-currents of emotion—and this crowd was more emotional than most.

"Are you all right?" Acton bent to ask her.

She nodded. Relax, she scolded herself; you're as tightly-wound as your husband. But—on reflection—she realized that this was no longer true. Ever since they'd figured-out Savoie's motives in this tangle, Acton had been much more relaxed, and he'd slept soundly through the night—even when she'd got up for the baby.

He's not having to break his word, she realized; he was steeling himself, before, because he thought what Savoie had done was inexcusable, and all debts of honor were therefore null and void. He's that relieved that the man didn't murder Howard—not necessarily because Acton has any friendly feelings toward Savoie, but because now he needn't break his promise. It was that medieval-mentality, rearing its strange and unfathomable head yet again.

As though on cue, the murmuring of the crowd increased in level and Doyle glanced back, to see that Mary had entered the courtroom—pale but composed—as Savoie ushered her toward their front-row seats beside Acton and Doyle.

Acton promptly stood, and greeted Mary kindly, taking both her hands in his which was very unusual for him. He then turned to Savoie and offered his hand. "Mr. Savoie; it is good to see you."

"*D'accord*," Savoie replied, as he accepted it.

A stand-down, thought Doyle, with immense relief. Good one, Doyle. And how things have turned around; rather than Acton's trying to keep Doyle away from the trial, now he'd joined her here, so as to publicly support the widow and tip the jury-scales in her favor.

Out of the corner of her eye, Doyle caught a glimpse of Mrs. Mackey, sitting with her knitting bag on her lap a few rows back. A very nice gesture, to come and support Mary, and Doyle waved a friendly greeting since the woman looked a bit overwhelmed.

The court clerk then asked everyone to rise as the judge entered to mount the bench, wearing his long wig and a solemn expression, as befit the occasion.

The trial began, and the audience listened intently to the prosecution's opening statement whist Doyle fought a feeling of bemusement; it was all a bit surreal, because the tale that was being told was only half the story—although none of the participants would ever know it.

Doyle's gaze rested on Sir Vikili's back, where he sat before them at the defendant's table. He's nowhere near as fashed as he was in Denisovich's office, she decided; good—another stand-down, courtesy of the fair Doyle.

She listened to his female co-counsel make her opening statement—a solicitor-advocate instead of a barrister, which was a bit unusual in so high-profile a case. She seemed a very capable woman, nonetheless—and besides, it could be presumed that Sir Vikiki wouldn't deign to work with anyone who wasn't top-drawer, especially in so important a case.

It seemed apparent from the woman's statement that the defense was going to concentrate on the element of "intent." To be held liable for a conspiracy to commit murder, the prosecution would have to show that every person who participated, had the specific intent to accomplish a murder, and—as the woman explained to the jury—the evidence would show that such was not the case.

"She's a fierce one," Doyle whispered to her husband.

"She is Melinda's solicitor," he advised.

Oh—thought Doyle; she must be the one that Acton had recommended to help Melinda in her fight against her erstwhile mother-in-law. Good one; she's a tigress, and no mistaking.

The prosecution called their first witness, the Coroner, to testify as to Nigel Howard's cause of death and confirm that an overdose of fentanyl was the culprit. Since the defense was not going to challenge him with a cross-examination, he was then excused to step down.

The prosecution then called Lizzie Williams, who laid-out in excruciating detail the chain-of-custody evidence and the lab findings of a fatal fentanyl dose, which had infiltrated a batch of over-the-counter medication purchased at New View Pharmacy by the various people who'd died.

Having established the mode of death, the prosecution than moved on to the manner of it, calling Ms. Piros—the transport company supervisor—to testify about the after-hours delivery to New View Pharmacy, which was made by the defendants under her supervision, along with her own suspicions when these same defendants had altered their time-cards so as to cover it up.

At the conclusion of her direct testimony, the defense's solicitor-advocate rose to cross-examine the supervisor—and since this would be the first challenge to the case that was being laid out —the crowd's interest sharpened. The cross-examination, however, did not go as anticipated.

Counsel asked, "You are originally from Pushkin, are you not?"

There was a small pause, whilst the supervisor considered this a bit warily. "Yes."

"The same town, I believe, as the late Sasha Lanska?"

As the witness stared at her, the Crown Prosecutor promptly rose to his feet; he wasn't about to allow his witness to be subject to a fishing expedition—especially one that might incite prejudices in the jury. "Objection; I fail to see the relevance, your honor."

"The question is withdrawn," the defense agreed. The woman then paused, facing the jury for dramatic effect, as she asked the witness, "You may be testifying for the Crown, Ms. Piros, but you first consulted with Sir Vikili, the defense solicitor, about the specifics of your testimony. Isn't that true?"

The witness sat, frozen.

Holy Mother, thought Doyle, as a loud wave of murmuring broke out in the courtroom and the judge called for order; the solicitor-advocate is throwing Sir Vikili under the bus, even though he's her flippin' co-counsel.

With some trepidation, Doyle watched for Sir Vikili's outraged reaction, but noted with some surprise that he continued to sit, unmoving.

Understandably shaken by the revelation that one of his witnesses had been conspiring with the defense, the Crown Prosecutor quickly rose to his feet. "Objection, your honor; if this witness sought legal advice such information would be privileged."

The judge, however, was thoroughly outraged by this implication of trial-tampering, and his brows drew down together. "The fact there was a meeting would not be privileged, counsel. I'll allow it." He then paused, to rest an accusing gaze on Sir Vikili, who appeared to be supremely unconcerned by the fact that he was about to be exposed as violating strict ethical rules.

Oh-ho, thought Doyle, as the penny dropped; I see Acton's fine hand, here. This witness is being made to walk the plank over Savoie-infested waters, and it seems that Sir Vikili is allowing it— as well as allowing the hit to his own reputation—because he owes Acton a favor. He can't betray this witness publicly, but he can stand aside, whilst she falls into the sea.

In an ominous tone, the judge instructed the witness, "You may answer."

"This is ridiculous," the witness blustered. "I'm not on trial, here." Despite herself, her gaze rested, for a panicked moment, on Savoie. "I'd like to confer with counsel."

The prosecutor was quick to suggest, "A side-bar, your honor—"

But the seasoned judge knew when a trial was about to blow-up in spectacular fashion, and only directed with awful emphasis, "Answer the question, if you please."

But an answer wasn't forthcoming, because the proceedings were suddenly interrupted when Mrs. Mackey pushed through the bar's gate and rushed the witness stand, wielding an ancient, heavy pistol, which she fired wildly at the witness.

As the startled court personnel ducked and scattered, the bailiffs converged upon the older woman, easily taking her to the floor and wrestling the weapon out of her hand.

"*Tiran!*" Mrs. Mackey shrieked at the horrified witness. "*Svolach!*"

"Order!" shouted the judge, as he banged his gavel in outrage.

CHAPTER 41

The trial was promptly adjourned, with the judge instructing the supervisor that she would be bound over for the next session, at a date to be determined.

There'll be no next session for her, Doyle thought, as she watched the woman scurry away; she's a marked woman.

Mrs. Mackey had been escorted back into the judge's chambers, and the judge had called Acton forward to consult as to how to proceed. When their meeting broke up, Acton approached Doyle and explained that he was going to arrest Mrs. Mackey, and take her into custody. "We'll need to clear the courtroom," he announced to those who'd stayed, hoping for some further excitement.

In a dignified manner, Sir Vikili rose to exit, and then bowed his head, slightly, as he paused before Savoie. "Sir," he said in a respectful tone. "May I expect you at my wedding?"

"*Peut-être,*" Savoie replied with a negligent shrug. "I am not one for the weddings."

This sentiment was proven false a few moments later, when

the Frenchman leaned down to say to Doyle in an aside, "You will come to my wedding, yes?"

"Willingly," she replied. "'Tis the eighth wonder of the world."

He smiled his thin smile. "*C'est dommage*, that I could not steal you from your husband, little bird."

Diplomatically, she didn't point out that she would never have agreed to such a scheme, and instead replied, "I think it's turned out better all around."

Doyle watched as he touched Mary's arm solicitously, to indicate that they should leave. It was all very symmetrical, in a strange way; Savoie had rescued the fair Doyle and now she'd rescued him right back—even though he'd probably never know it. And she'd saved Mary as well, just as Howard's ghost had asked; no one would dare go after Gemma, now that the notorious Philippe Savoie was going to marry the girl's mother.

I never saw *any* of this, comin', Doyle admitted to herself. Which is why it's a good thing that I'm not the one who's in charge.

Of course, she was firmly hoist on the horns of her usual dilemma; murder was murder, no matter how just the cause, and she was a sworn law enforcement officer. But try as she might, she could see no other way out of this particular moral dilemma. A rough sort of justice had been served-up by people who had little respect for the formal justice system, in the first place. The police saw this sort of thing a lot, truth to tell—mainly because the formal justice system often missed the mark, or was seen to be stacked against ordinary people. It was a dangerous thing, though, because vigilantism had its own evils—you didn't want to encourage a system where might made right, instead of the other way 'round.

Her thoughts were interrupted by Acton, who said to her, "I

would like to interview Mrs. Mackey, if you would accompany me, please."

"Lead on," she said easily.

She suspicioned that the reason he was so keen to interview Mrs. Mackey on the spot—instead of back at headquarters—was because he was going to do a bit of damage control. The last needful thing would be for the truth of this little tale to be made public—not to mention the troubling little fact that the attempted murderess had acted as the House of Acton's housekeeper, in recent days.

Doyle accompanied her husband back into the judge's chambers, where Mrs. Mackey sat looking rather defiant, with the bailiffs and the judge standing at a small distance and keeping a wary eye on her.

Doyle wondered, for a moment, if Acton would want to clear out the others; if he was going to manipulate things so as to keep her motives quiet, best that there be no witnesses—but he didn't seemed concerned, as he pulled up a chair and sat facing the witness.

"Your name, please?"

"Irena Macogonova," she replied.

"Could you tell me where you hail from, Mrs. Macogonova?"

"I am from Novocherkassk," the woman declared, with a touch of defiance.

"And why did you attempt to shoot at Mrs. Piros?"

"A godless *bolo*," Mrs. Mackey retorted in an angry tone. "Plotting with that harlot, to make another little martyr—"

"*Molchat*, I would suggest," Acton interrupted in a mild tone. "Calmly, please."

The woman stared at him for a long moment, before she lowered her gaze and nodded.

Acton continued, "I believe you killed Miss Valerie Cervena."

Doyle glanced at him in surprise, as the woman lifted her chin and readily admitted, "I did. Another blasphemer—that one was easy, but I didn't quite know how to manage this one."

"Who gave you the weapon?"

"It was my father's. He was killed in the uprising, when I was a young girl." She paused. "He would be very proud."

"How did you smuggle the gun through security?"

Rather pleased, the woman explained, "I wrapped it in my knitting wool, and then when the alarm went off I told them it was my knitting needles that did it."

Acton nodded, and then rose. "I will call for a field unit, to take her into custody."

"You may do as you wish, with your jackbooted *Cheka*," Mrs. Mackey declared in righteous defiance. "A crown in heaven awaits me."

"You know," Doyle observed, "You remind me of a deacon I once knew."

CHAPTER 42

*T*hey'd returned home, and—after having put the boys down—Doyle was seated at the kitchen table, watching Reynolds with some bemusement as he cautiously peered into the oven.

"When's the last time you baked *me* a cake?" she asked, rather pointedly.

"I've always wanted to attempt a *medovic*," the butler replied, unashamed. "I hope it turns out." He was baking the confection to bring to Mrs. Mackey, where she was being held in Detention.

"I don't know as they'll let you bring it in," Doyle advised. "They'll think you've hidden a file within it."

"Lord Acton assures me there will be no problem, madam."

She's a hero to both of them, thought Doyle. And who's to say they're wrong, save that murder is a mortal sin—even vigilante murders, which always seem to be thick on the ground around here.

And, hard on this thought, she pushed her chair out, deciding it was past time to wander downstairs so as to discuss these matters with her husband—she figured she'd given him ample time to decompress, and sort himself out.

As could be expected, Acton was seated in his office, cradling a glass of scotch and gazing out the windows.

He looked up, when she closed the door. "You were right," he said.

"I'm afraid you'll have to be more specific," she teased.

"I was not paying proper attention. In fact, I missed something rather obvious—the aliases that the conspirators used."

She walked over to stand behind him, and fondly run her hands along his shoulders. "What's this?"

"Mrs. Rossa, Mrs. Cervena, Mrs. Piros. All mean "red" in different languages."

Doyle raised her brows. "Red, for the Bolsheviks?"

"Yes." He reached to clasp one of her hands with his own, where it rested on his shoulder. "Well done."

She winced. "I don't know, husband; there's a crackin' big body-count, for 'well done'. What's goin' to happen to Mrs. Mackey?"

"Aggravated assault, I imagine. Due to her age, she'll probably wind-up in Wexton minimum security."

She began gently massaging his shoulders as she eyed the top of his head. "I noticed that you didn't read her the caution, before you asked her to confess to Miss Valerie's murder."

He tilted his head. "I must have forgot," he said, and it was a lie.

"Well, there's no sweepin' such a lapse under the rug, what with the judge there as witness."

"I imagine you are correct," he agreed, wholly unashamed.

"What was it, that you said to her? She was about to start gabblin' about Gemma, but then she quieted right down."

He explained, "The term *molchat* was a byword for the Russian citizens under the Soviets. It means "keep silence," and refers to matters that are best kept quiet, for fear of reprisal."

"No one grasses on each other," Doyle agreed. "We've somethin' similar, in Ireland. D'you think she'll keep the silence?"

"I would imagine," he replied. "She's had a lot of practice."

Thinking about this, she absently continued her massage. "She signed-on as our housekeeper because she thought Miss Valerie would be there—she was that surprised, that we didn't bring a nanny."

"I would imagine. I wonder how she found out about the plot?"

"Recall that the plotters met at the ROC, here in town, and she was a parishioner. She must have overheard somethin'."

He raised his brows. "The church was a good cover, you must admit."

"I'll agree with Mrs. Mackey—wretched blasphemers, to so misuse a House of God."

She knit her brow as she continued working his shoulders. "Faith, Michael; why on earth didn't she just tell us about what these terrible people were plottin'? She'd plenty of opportunity."

"We are the police," her husband explained. "She believes—from long experience—that you don't dare trust the police."

She leaned down, and looped her arms 'round his neck so that her cheek rested against his. "Small wonder that you're drinkin', husband. You missed the boat, on this one. Faith, I'm the one who should be drinkin', from always havin' to save you from yourself."

He placed a fond hand on her arm. "I will admit that I was far too focused on my objective."

"Blinded by wrath," she agreed. "I'd say 'let this be a lesson', but I think that goes without sayin'."

"Yes."

She squeezed him, fondly. "Good on you, Michael, for withdrawin' from the field and forsakin' the battle. I know it wasn't easy."

He made no response, and she thought she may as well point out, "Although, after this little holy-show at the trial, all the local villains are goin' to think you were a part of Savoie's scorched-earth campaign from the start—even though you were just as clueless as I was."

"It does not hurt, to allow the players to believe I was involved."

Making a sound of disapproval, she said into his ear, "You shouldn't be lookin' for street cred, my friend. You're supposed to be enforcin' the law."

"Mutual fear is what keeps everyone in line," he pointed out reasonably.

"Mutual goodwill and trust," she countered.

"A little of both," he compromised, and she found that she couldn't disagree.

Idly, her fingers started tracing his chest. "Speakin' of such, what will happen to Sir Vikili?"

"Perhaps an admonishment, at worst. Note that the witness never answered the question about his advising her."

"Well, good on Sir Vikili, for cooperatin' with your little holy-show."

"He owed me."

"I prefer to think it was the fruit of good works, Michael. And I was thinkin' about it; if Javid painted Sasha's portrait, it stands to reason that Javid got a pretty good read on what made the woman tick—she's one who knows how to see into people."

"A good point," he agreed thoughtfully. "Or perhaps Sasha trusted Javid enough to say something outright, about the thwarted plan to go after Gemma, and Howard's death."

Doyle paused in her stroking circuit. "Aye. Which would also explain why Sir Vikili couldn't say anythin' to you outright; Sasha would know that Javid was the one who'd grassed her out."

"Indeed."

With all admiration, Doyle observed, "Faith, if that's the case, Javid definitely deserves the sapphire necklace."

"You were never one for jewelry," her husband noted with some regret.

She smiled. "I am one for saints, though. Let's donate one of those fancy gold icons to the Russian Orthodox Church—a saint who's a proper martyr, so as to counter the more questionable ones."

"A very good idea. Which saint?"

"Their priest can decide—he'd know which would be best."

She then decided that more direct action was needed, and so she circled the chair to climb onto his lap, astraddle, and rest her arms on his shoulders so that her face was close to his. "Williams said that a man can always tell when a woman is givin' him the green light. Is that true?" She planted a soft kiss on his cheek.

Amused, he replied, "I would rate it as true."

She narrowed her eyes. "How many women give you the green light, in the course of an average day?"

"None that can hold a candle to you."

Laughing, she declared, "Faith, but you're a smooth one."

Very content, he closed his eyes as she resumed placing leisurely kisses along his face. "D'you know, husband, when I'm givin' you the green light?"

"I do."

Gently, she bit his ear. "I don't think you do."

"I believe you are leaking."

"Oh," she said, straightening up and observing the stains on her best blouse. "*So annoyin'.*"

"I never cared for this tie, anyway."

She laughed, and leaned down to nuzzle him. "Don't move; I'll go grab Tommy and be back in a few."

"I will come along, and supervise," he decided, as he rose to his feet.

"Don't be pushin' poor Tommy out of the way," she warned.

"There's plenty to go around," he replied easily, as he steered her down the hallway.

"Aye, aye, sir," she teased. "Hence."

9 798986 211527